FAR OUT
FABLES

STONE ARCH BOOKS
a capstone imprint

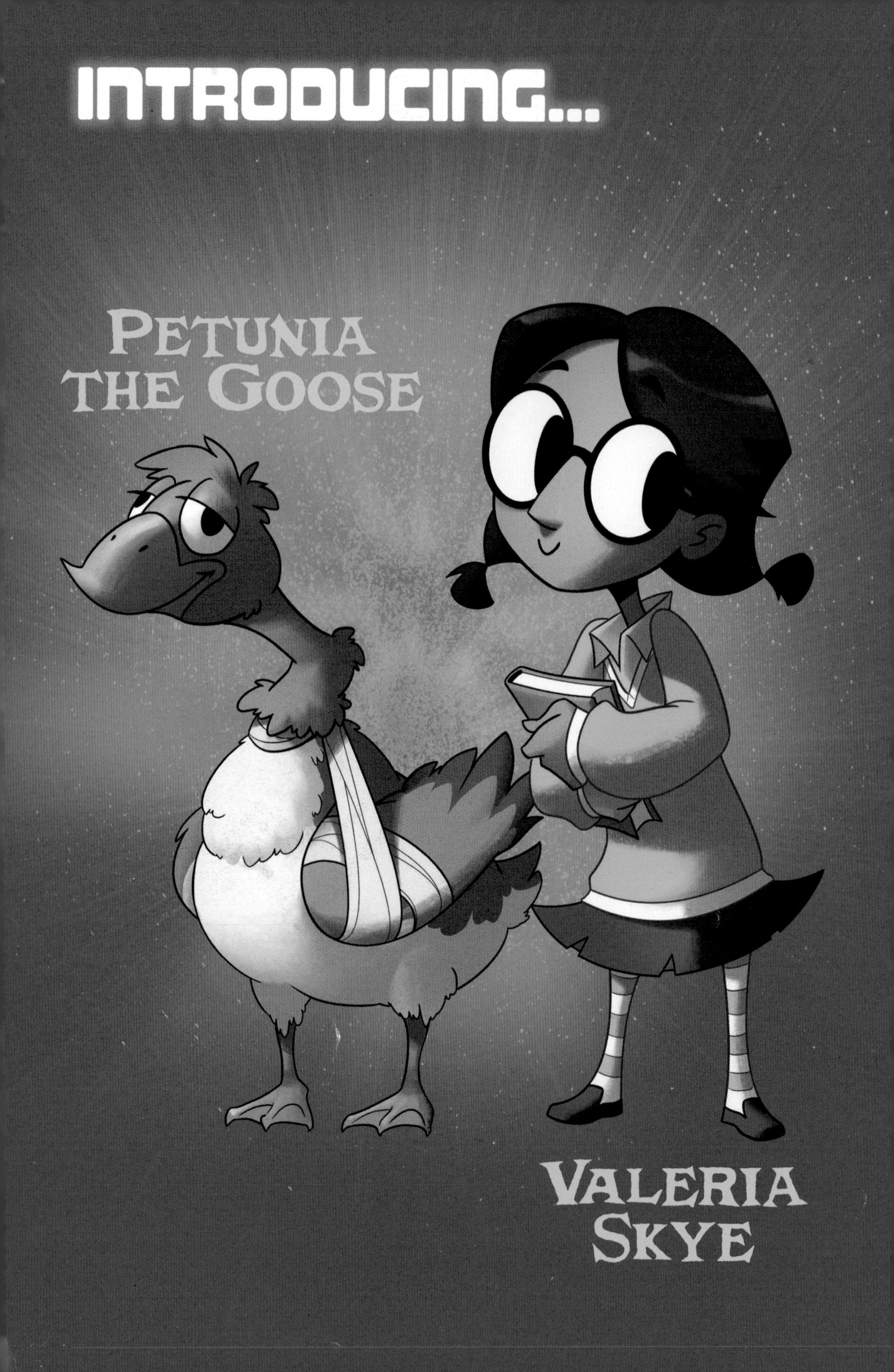
INTRODUCING...
PETUNIA THE GOOSE
VALERIA SKYE

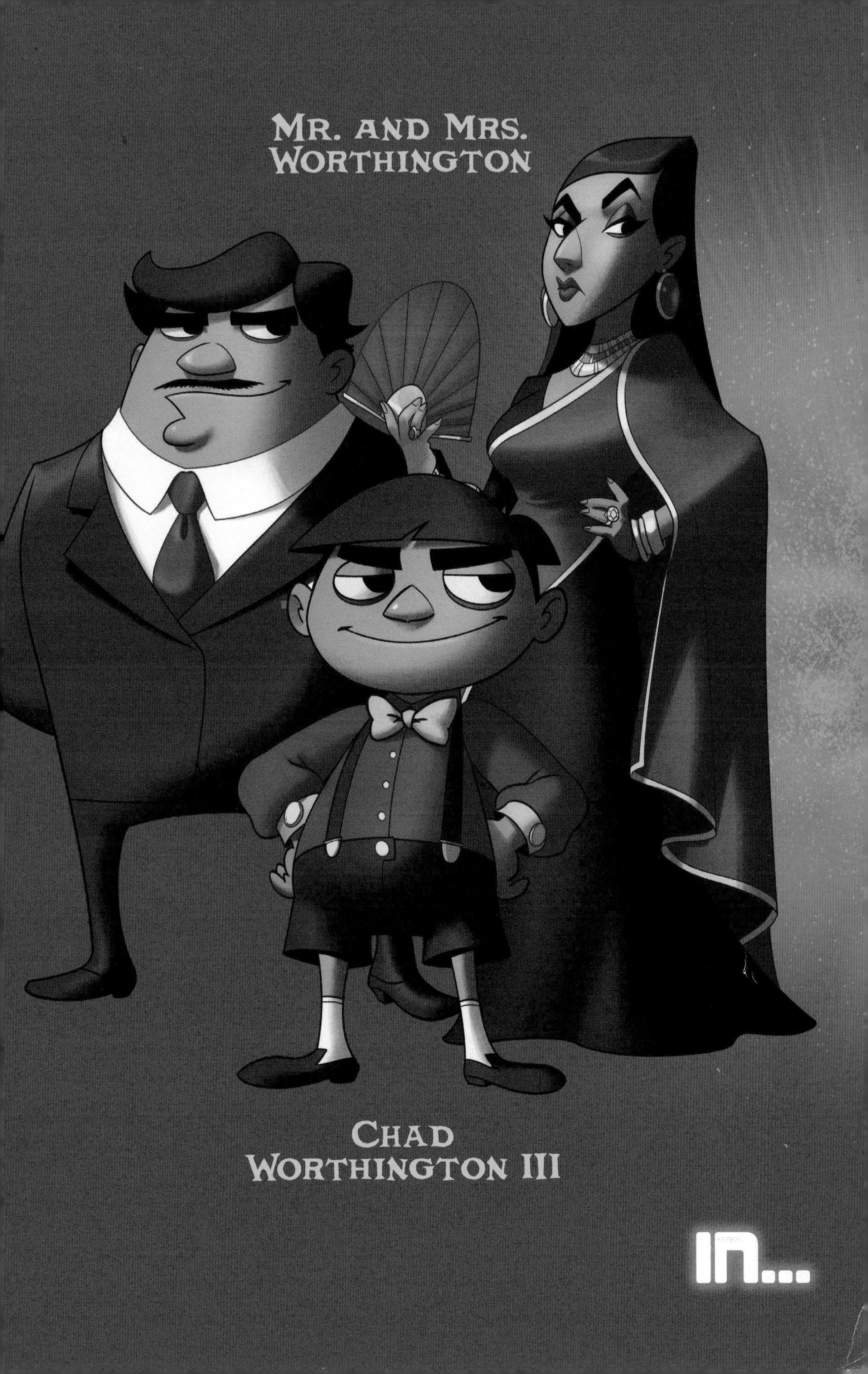
MR. AND MRS.
WORTHINGTON
CHAD
WORTHINGTON III
IN...

Far Out Fables is published by
Stone Arch Books,
an imprint of Capstone.
1710 Roe Crest Drive
North Mankato, Minnesota 56003
www.capstonepub.com

Cataloging-in-Publication Data is
available at the Library of Congress
website.

ISBN 978-1-5158-8218-3 (hardcover)
ISBN 978-1-5158-8327-2 (paperback)
ISBN 978-1-5158-9242-7 (eBook PDF)

Summary: A goose can lay golden eggs,
but when the wealthy Worthingtons
try to force them out, the eggs are
different. Smellier. They're ROTTEN!
But the greedy family will do anything
to get the gold and make a fortune.
Will the goose be able fly the coop
and escape?

Designed by Hilary Wacholz
Edited by Abby Huff
Lettered by Jaymes Reed

Printed and bound in the United States of America. PO3837

FAR OUT FABLES

THE GOOSE THAT LAID THE ROTTEN EGG

A GRAPHIC NOVEL

BY STEVE FOXE

ILLUSTRATED BY FERN CANO

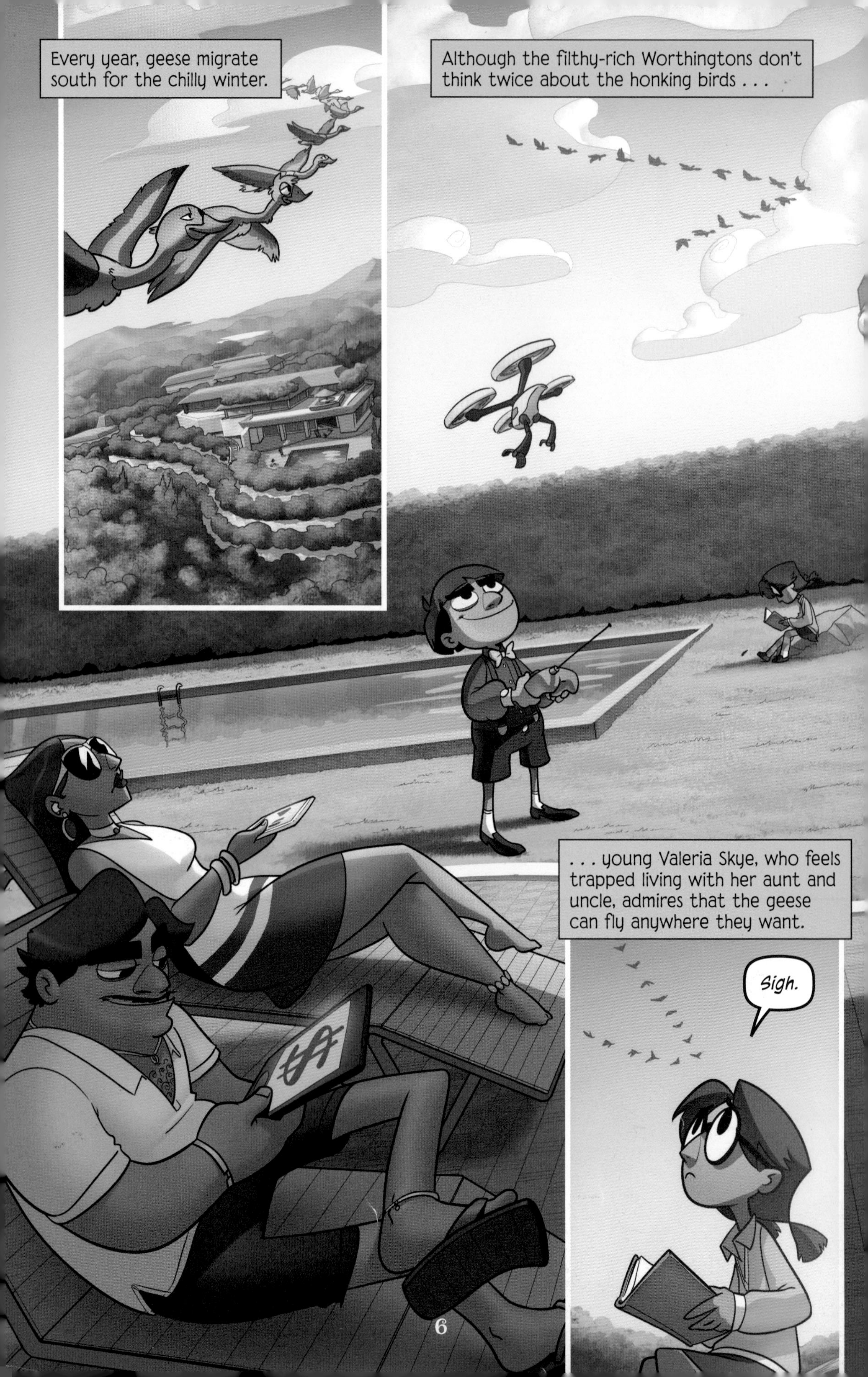
Every year, geese migrate south for the chilly winter.
Although the filthy-rich Worthingtons don't think twice about the honking birds . . .
. . . young Valeria Skye, who feels trapped living with her aunt and uncle, admires that the geese can fly anywhere they want.
Sigh.

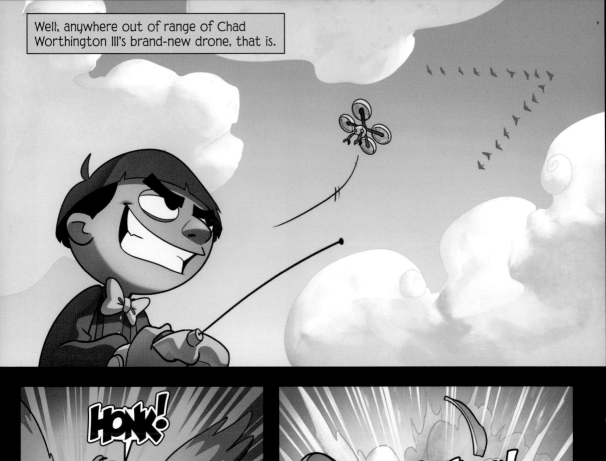

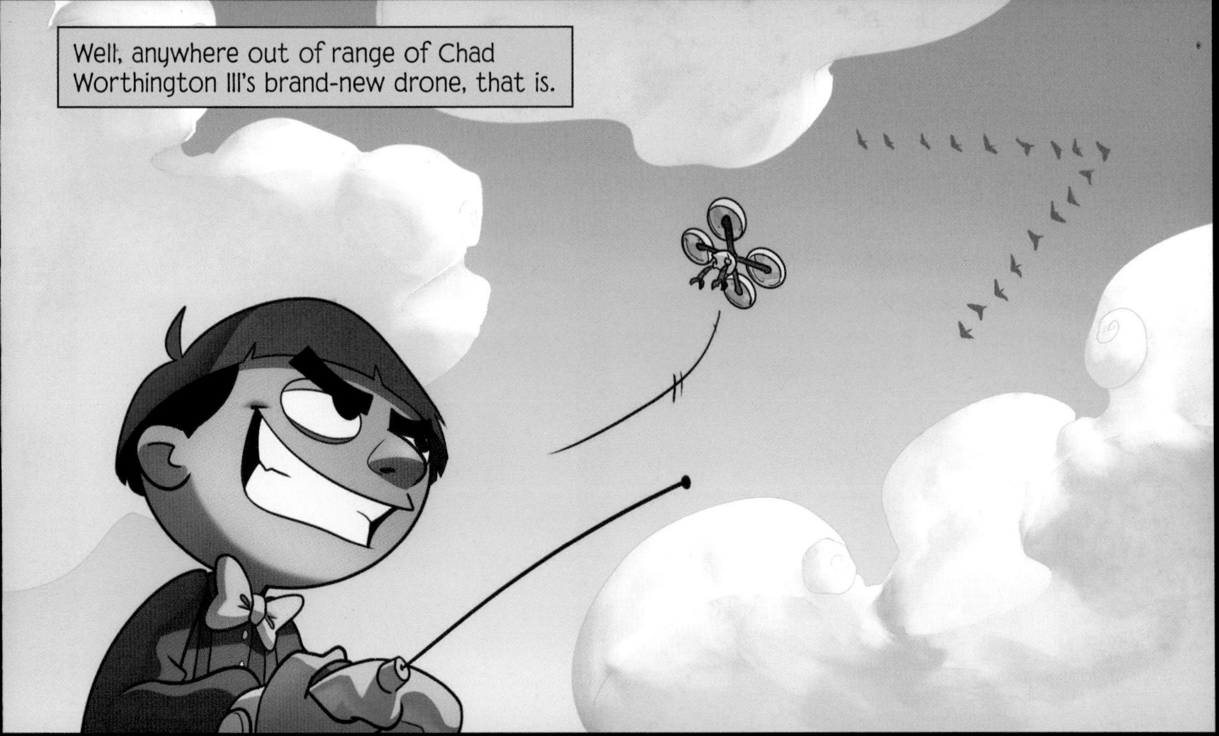
Well, anywhere out of range of Chad Worthington III's brand-new drone, that is.

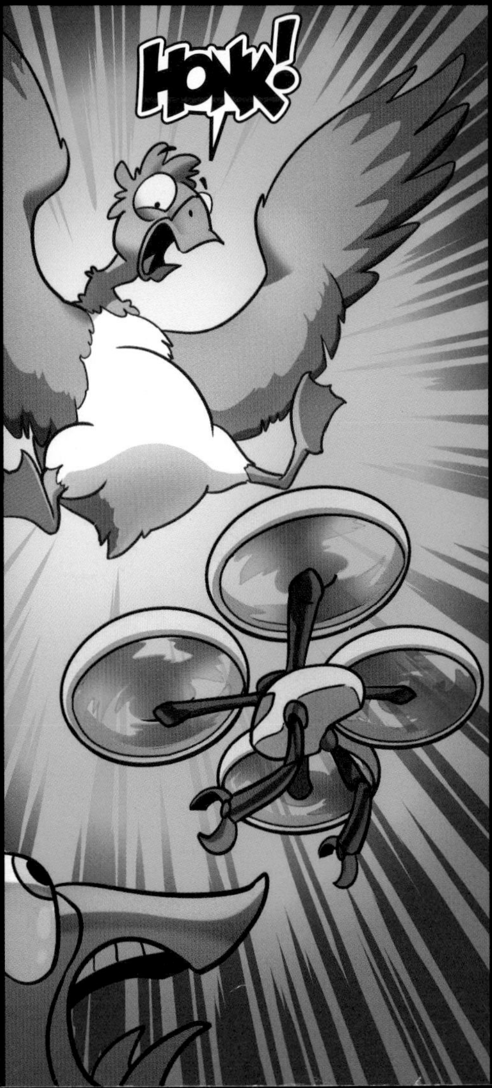
HONK!

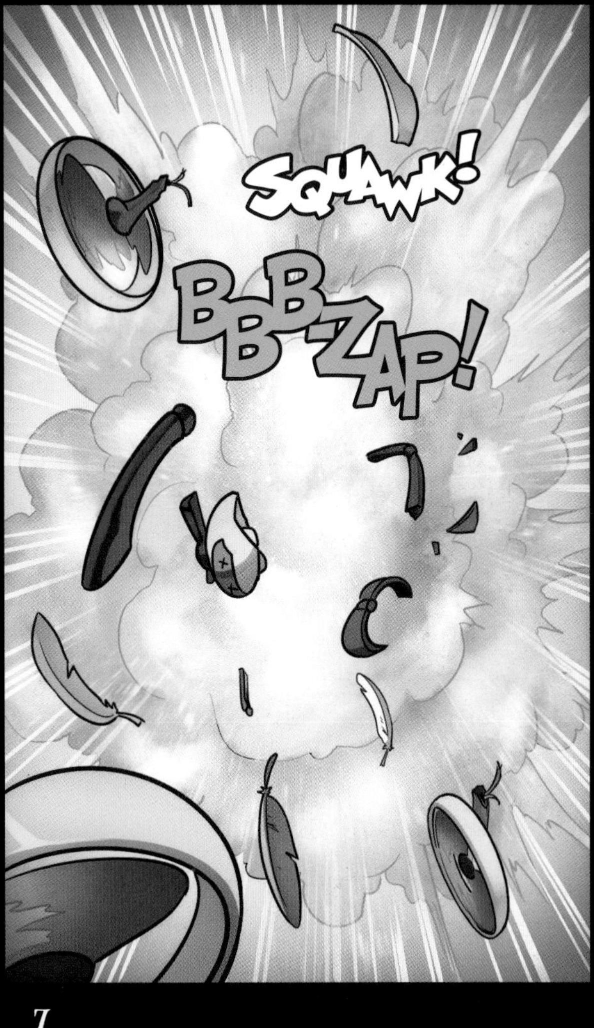
SQUAWK!
BBBZAP!

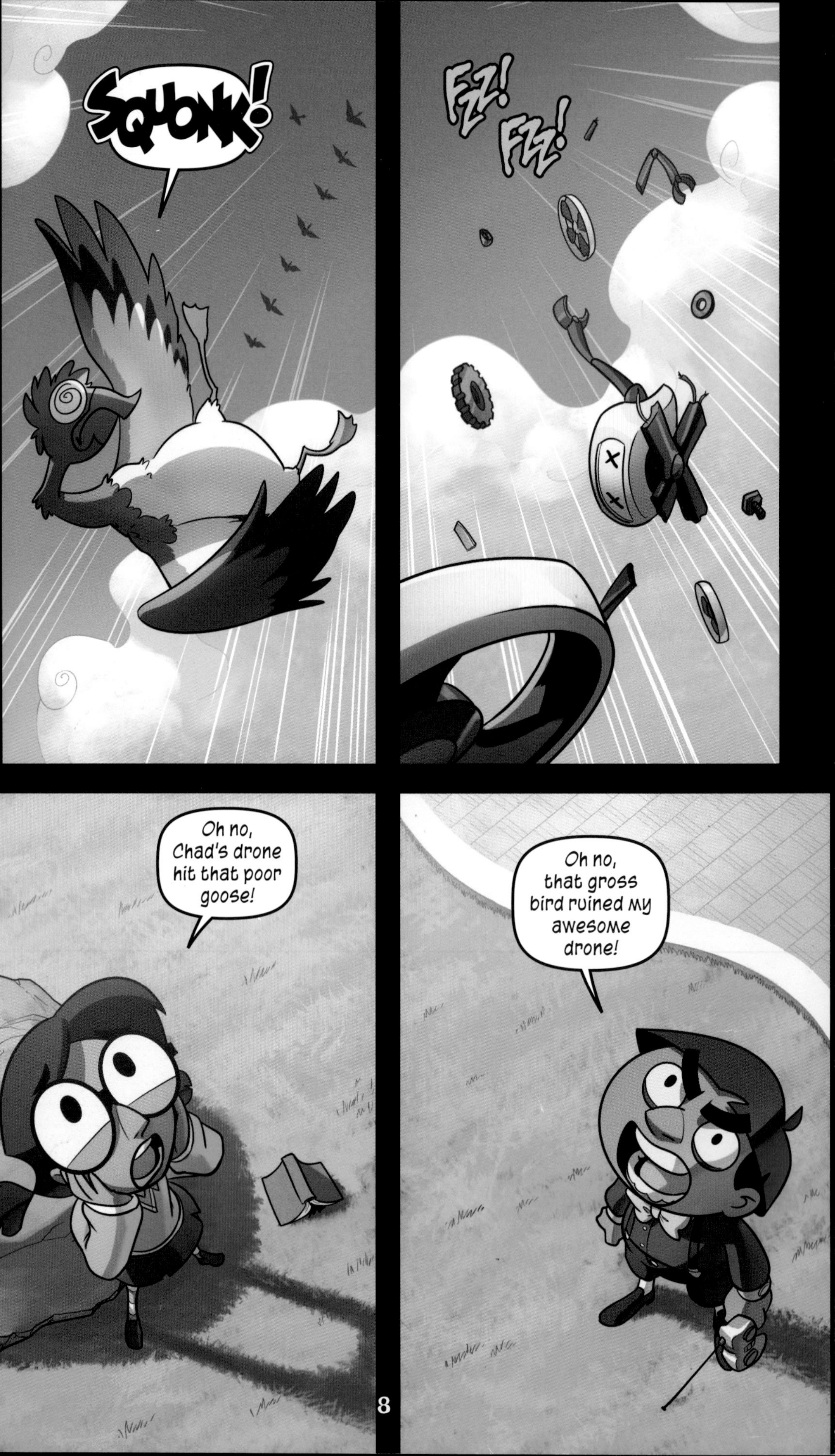
SQUONK!
FZZ! FZZ!
Oh no, Chad's drone hit that poor goose!
Oh no, that gross bird ruined my awesome drone!

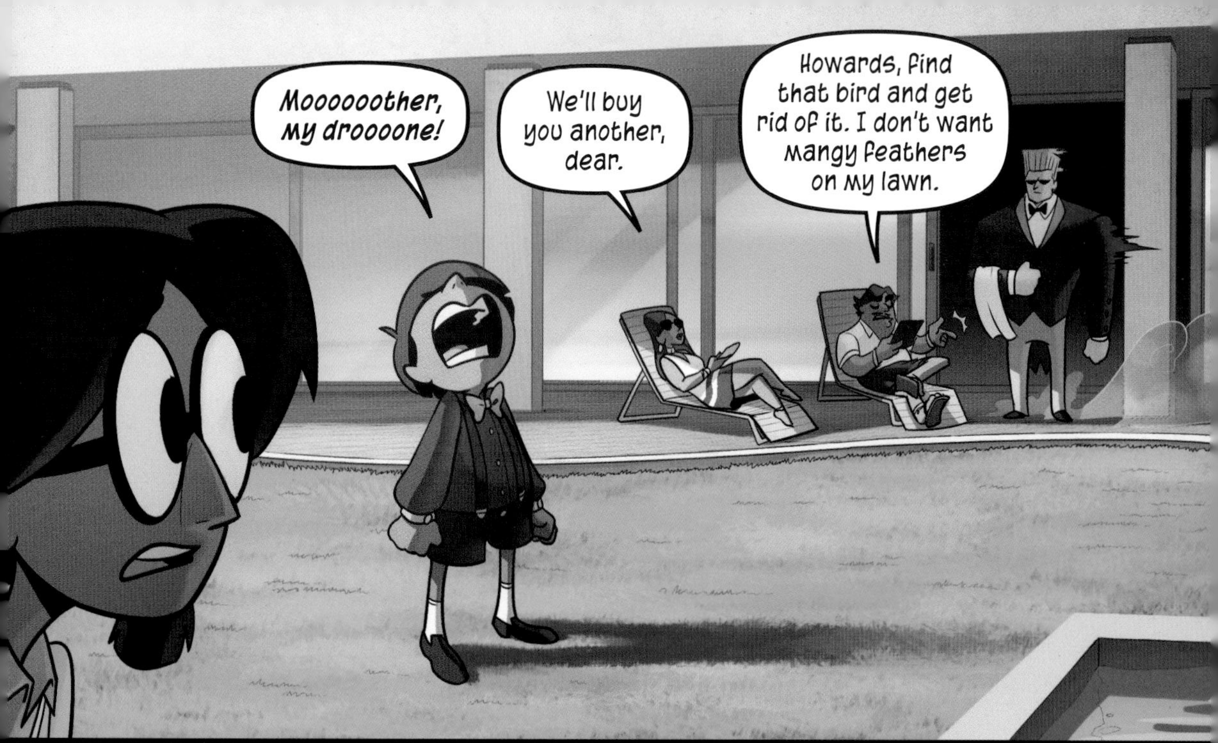
Moooooother, my droooone!
We'll buy you another, dear.
Howards, find that bird and get rid of it. I don't want mangy feathers on my lawn.

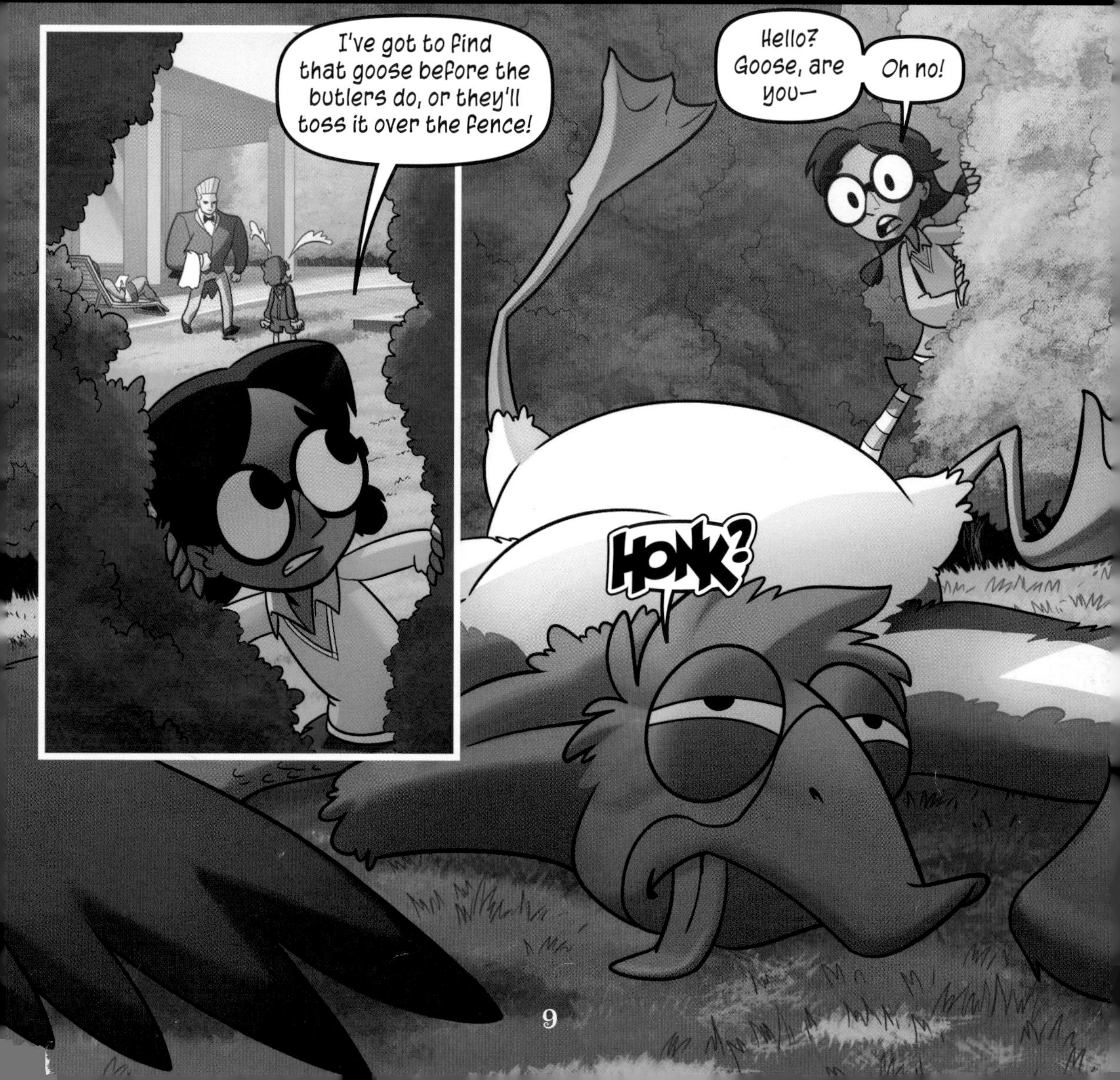
I've got to find that goose before the butlers do, or they'll toss it over the fence!
Hello? Goose, are you—
Oh no!
HONK?

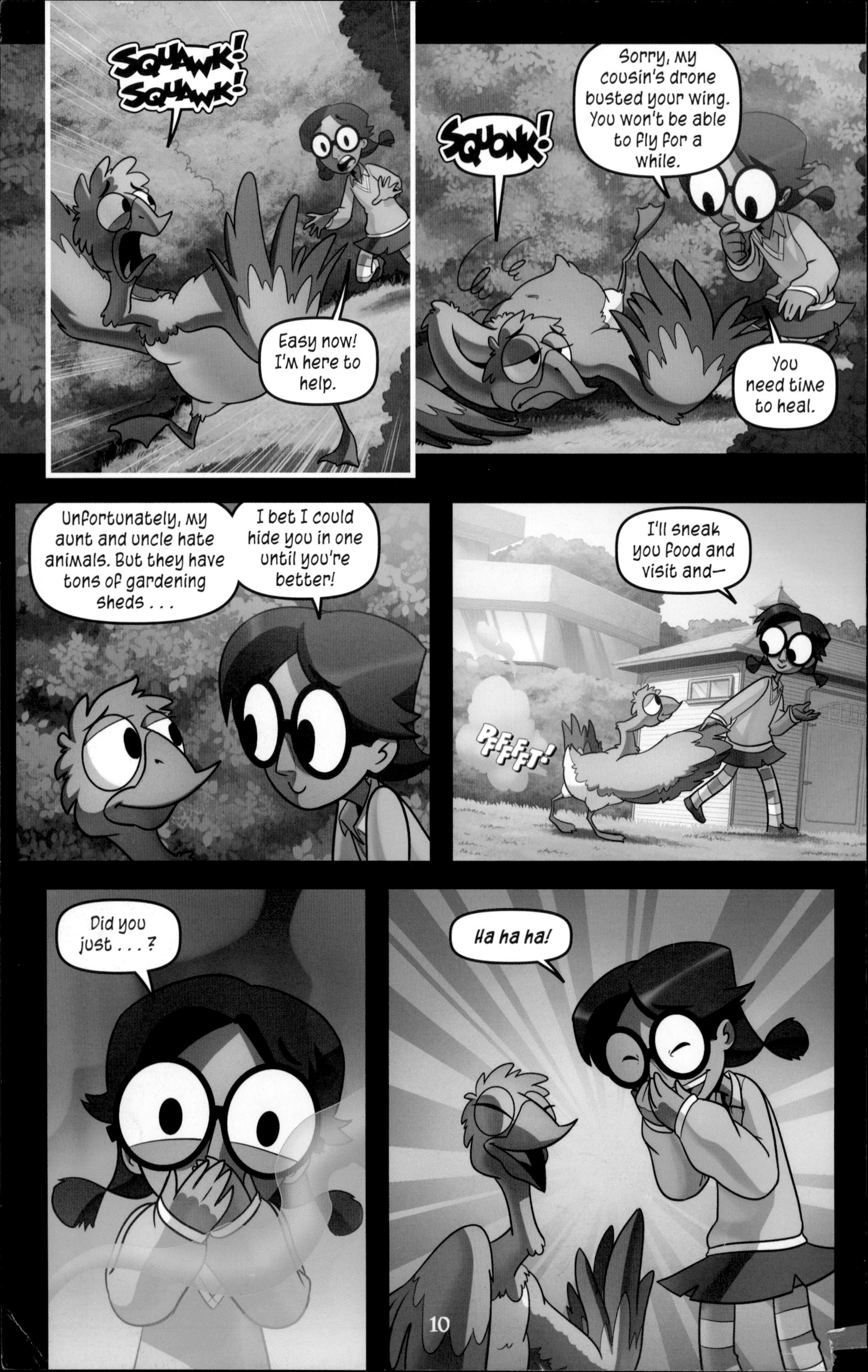
SQUAWK! SQUAWK!
Easy now! I'm here to help.
SQUONK!
Sorry, my cousin's drone busted your wing. You won't be able to fly for a while.
You need time to heal.
Unfortunately, my aunt and uncle hate animals. But they have tons of gardening sheds . . .
I bet I could hide you in one until you're better!
I'll sneak you food and visit and—
PFFFFT!
Did you just . . . ?
Ha ha ha!

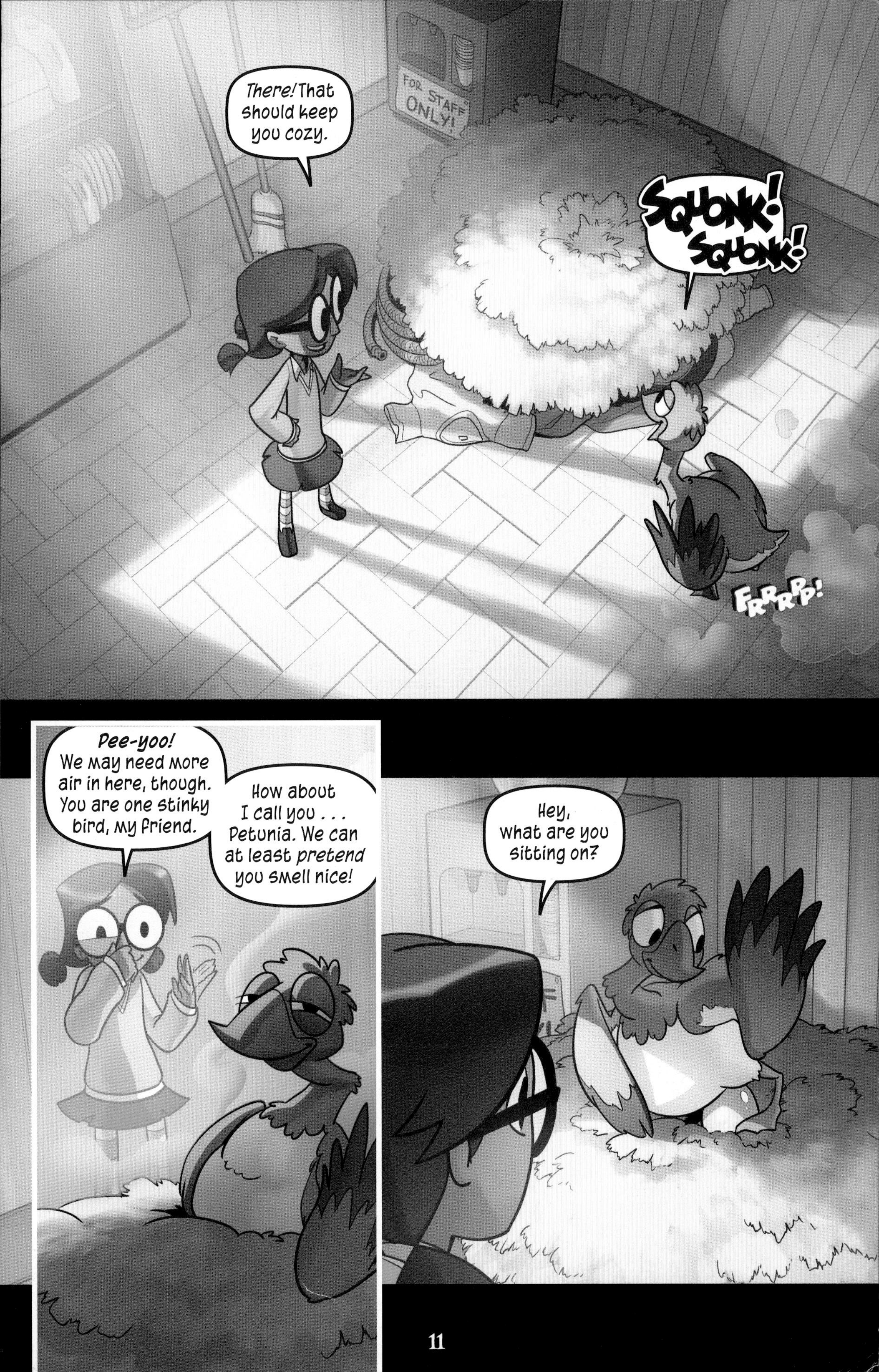
There! That should keep you cozy.
SQUONK! SQUONK!
FRRRPP!
Pee-yoo! We may need more air in here, though. You are one stinky bird, my friend.
How about I call you . . . Petunia. We can at least *pretend* you smell nice!
Hey, what are you sitting on?
FOR STAFF ONLY!

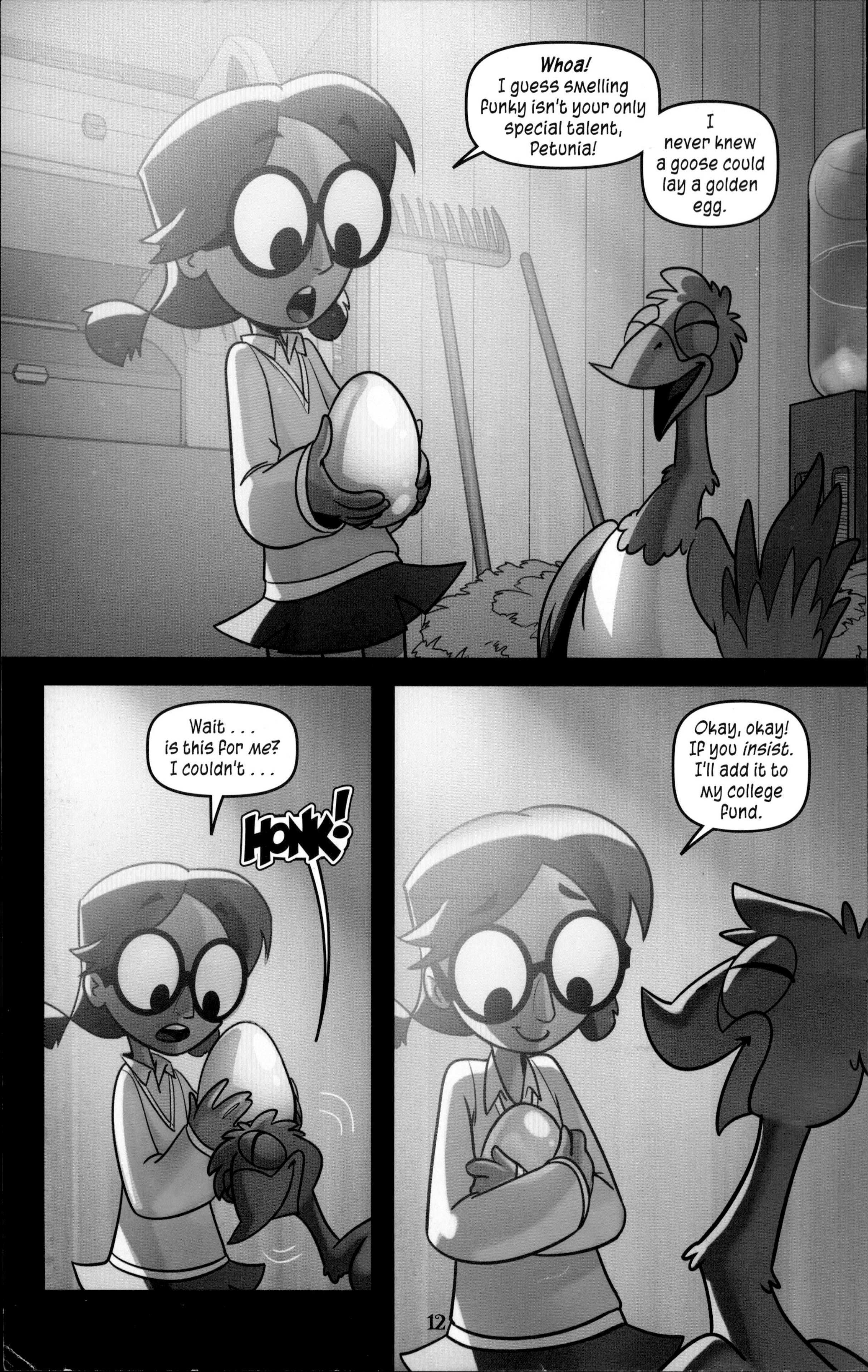
Whoa! I guess smelling funky isn't your only special talent, Petunia!
I never knew a goose could lay a golden egg.
Wait . . . is this for me? I couldn't . . .
HONK!
Okay, okay! If you insist. I'll add it to my college fund.

As the weeks went by, Valeria secretly cared for Petunia. Every few days, the goose laid a solid-gold egg.

PFFFFT!

And every *single* day, the goose passed gas. But Valeria didn't mind.

This might have continued until Petunia's wing had fully healed, if not for . . .

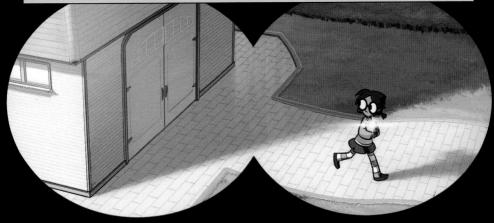

. . . *Chad.*

Do I spy something *shiny?*

Mother! Father! Valeria has something I don't!

Oh my. We can't have that, can we, dear?

The next day . . .

Hey! Give that back!

WHOOSH!

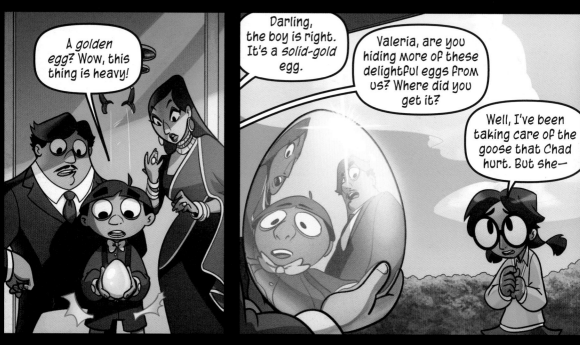

A golden egg? Wow, this thing is heavy!

Darling, the boy is right. It's a solid-gold egg.

Valeria, are you hiding more of these delightful eggs from us? Where did you get it?

Well, I've been taking care of the goose that Chad hurt. But she—

Quickly, Howards. Find the bird. Bring it inside so we can easily collect the eggs.

And gather any Valeria has tucked away.

SNAP!

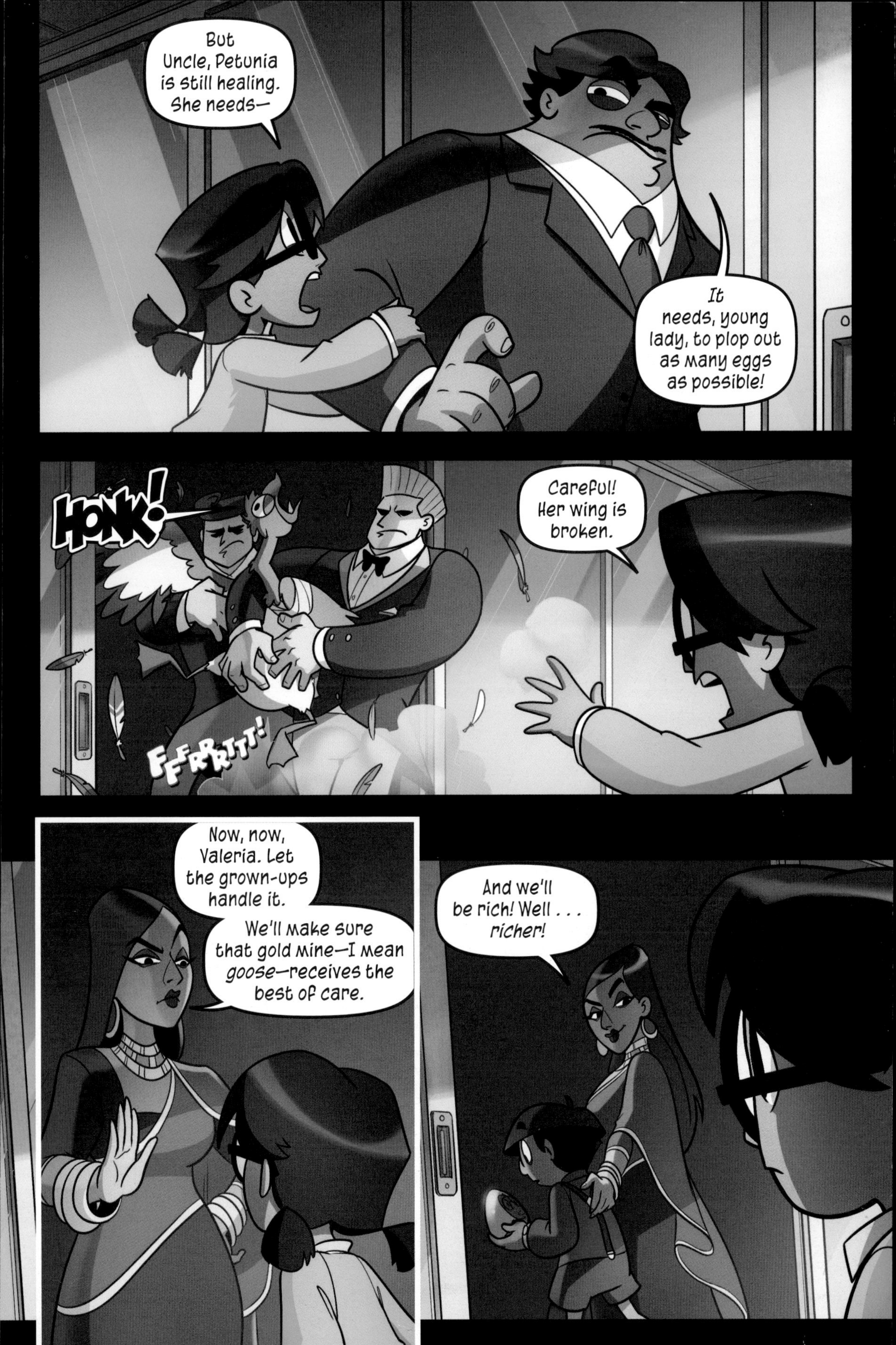
But Uncle, Petunia is still healing. She needs—
It needs, young lady, to plop out as many eggs as possible!
HONK!
FFRRRTTT!
Careful! Her wing is broken.
Now, now, Valeria. Let the grown-ups handle it.
We'll make sure that gold mine—I mean *goose*—receives the best of care.
And we'll be rich! Well . . . *richer!*

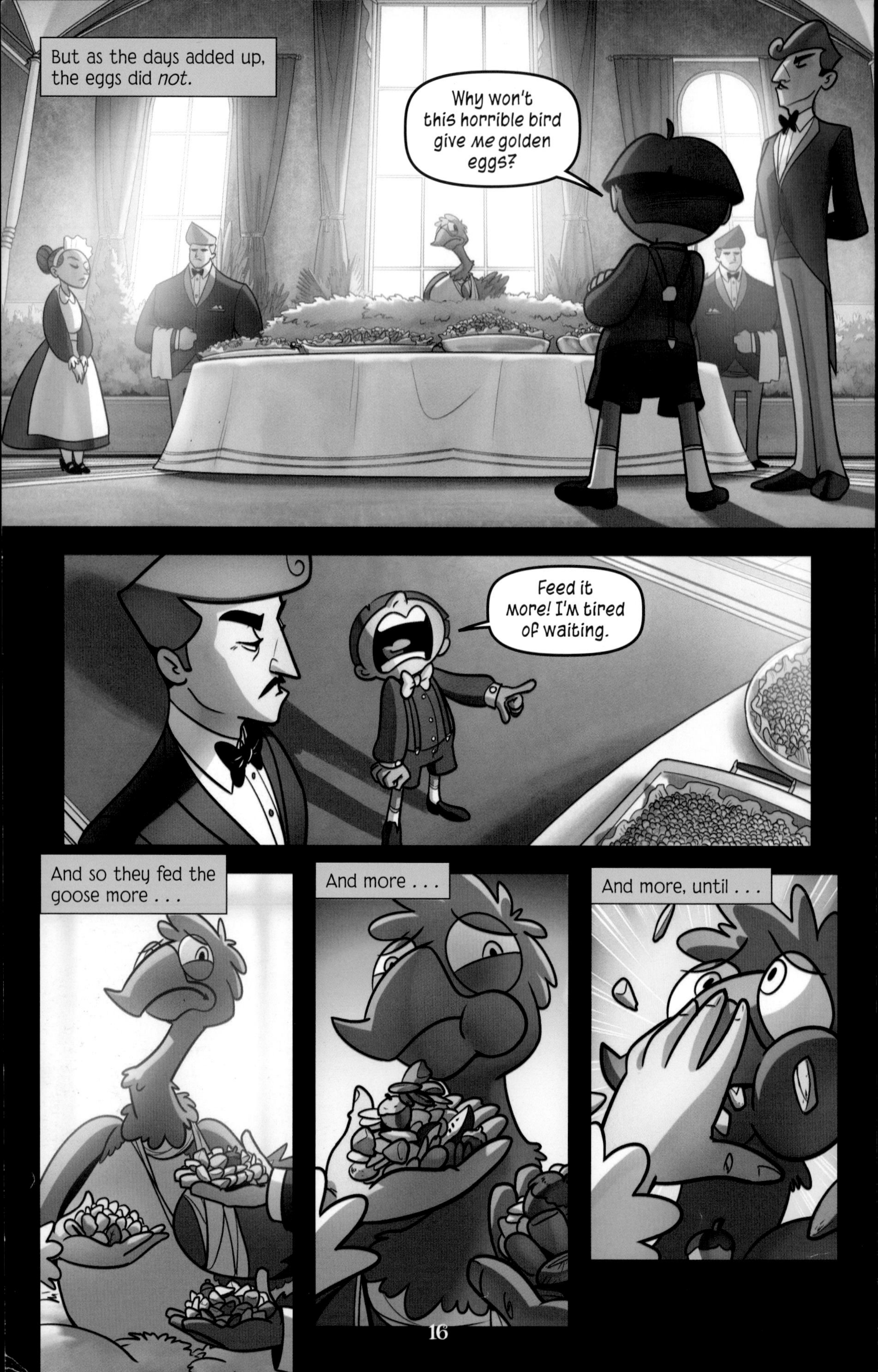
But as the days added up, the eggs did *not*.
Why won't this horrible bird give *me* golden eggs?
Feed it more! I'm tired of waiting.
And so they fed the goose more . . .
And more . . .
And more, until . . .

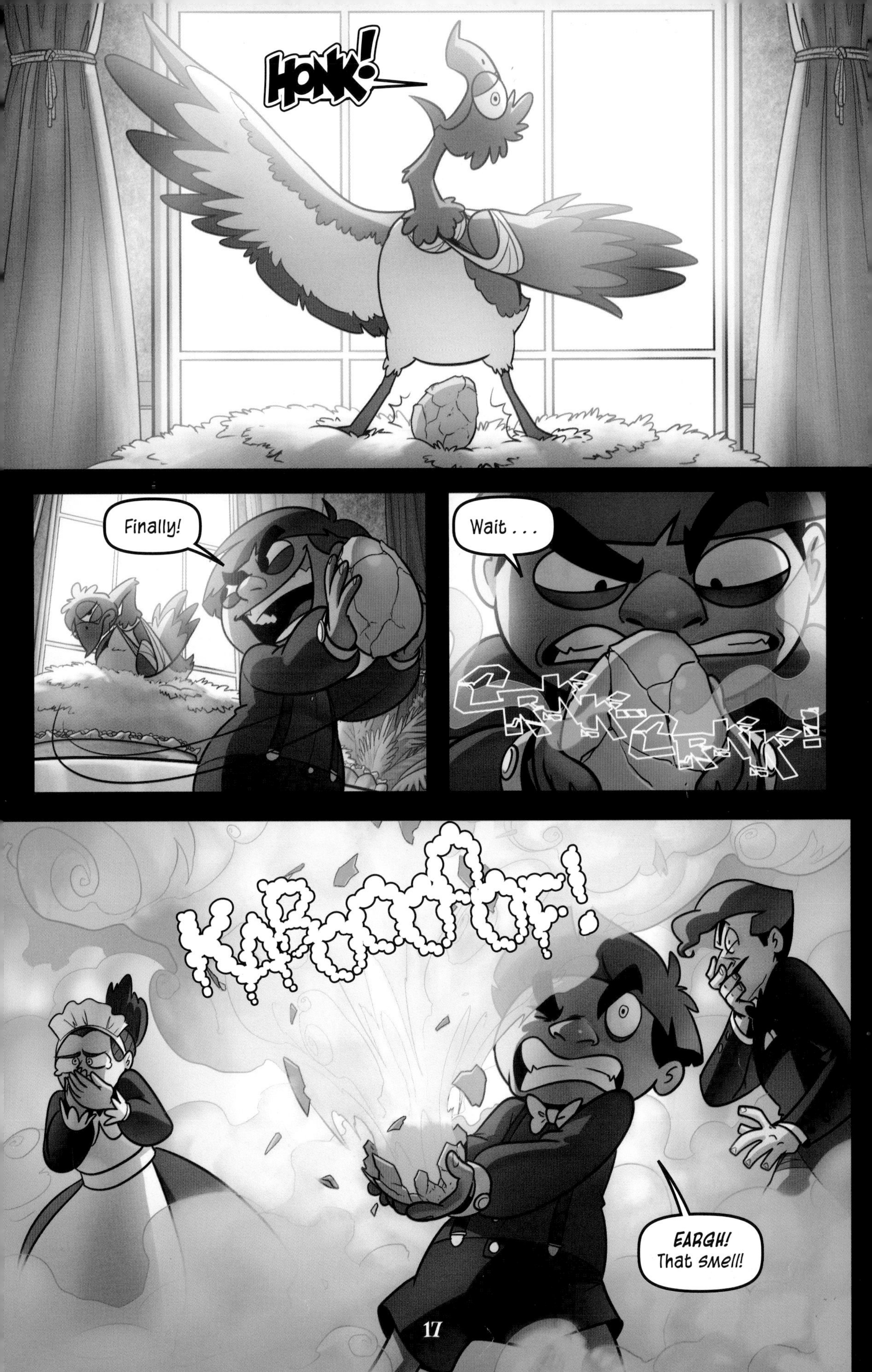
HONK!
Finally!
Wait . . .
CRK-CRK-CRK!
KABOOOOOF!
EARGH! That smell!

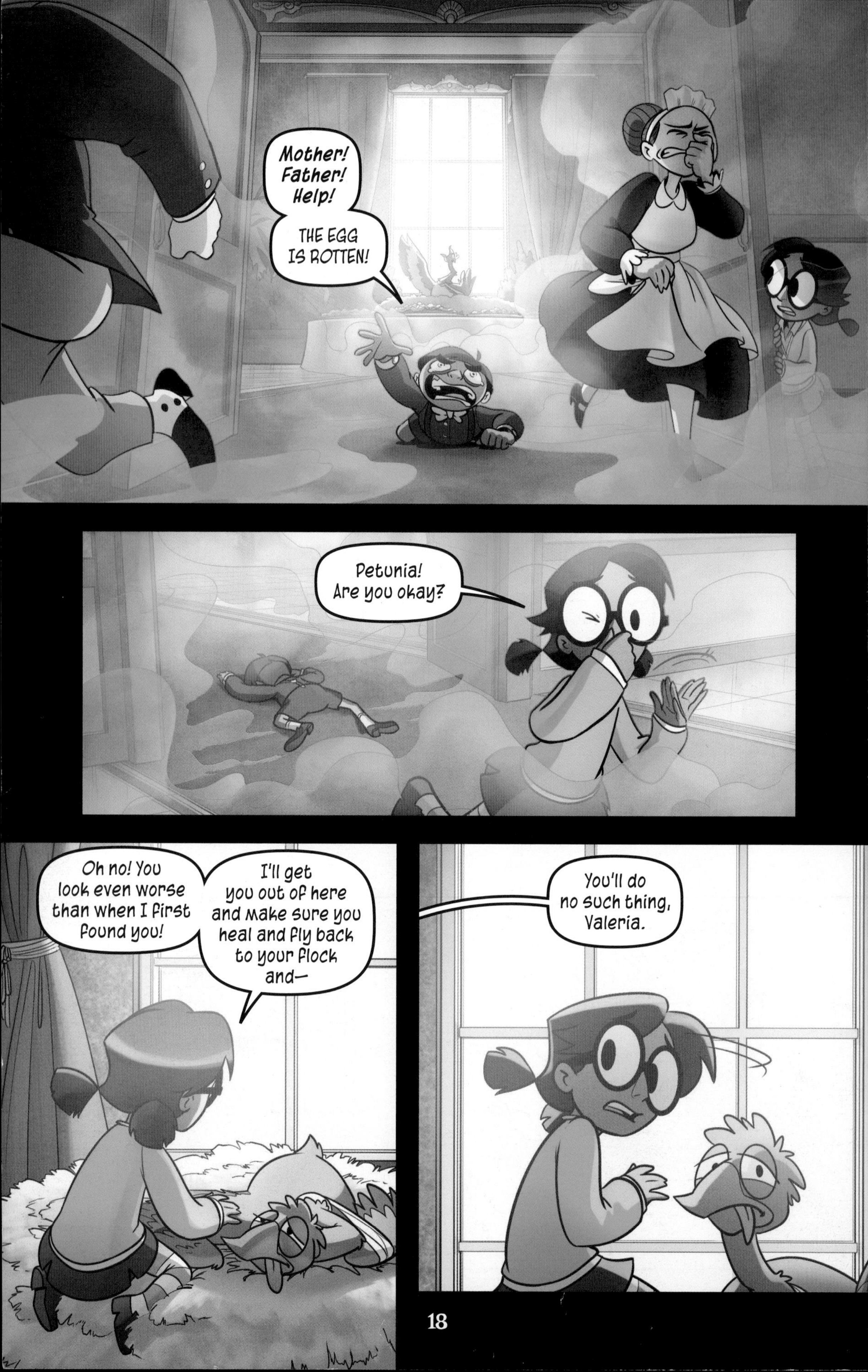
Mother! Father! Help!
THE EGG IS ROTTEN!
Petunia! Are you okay?
Oh no! You look even worse than when I first found you!
I'll get you out of here and make sure you heal and fly back to your flock and—
You'll do no such thing, Valeria.

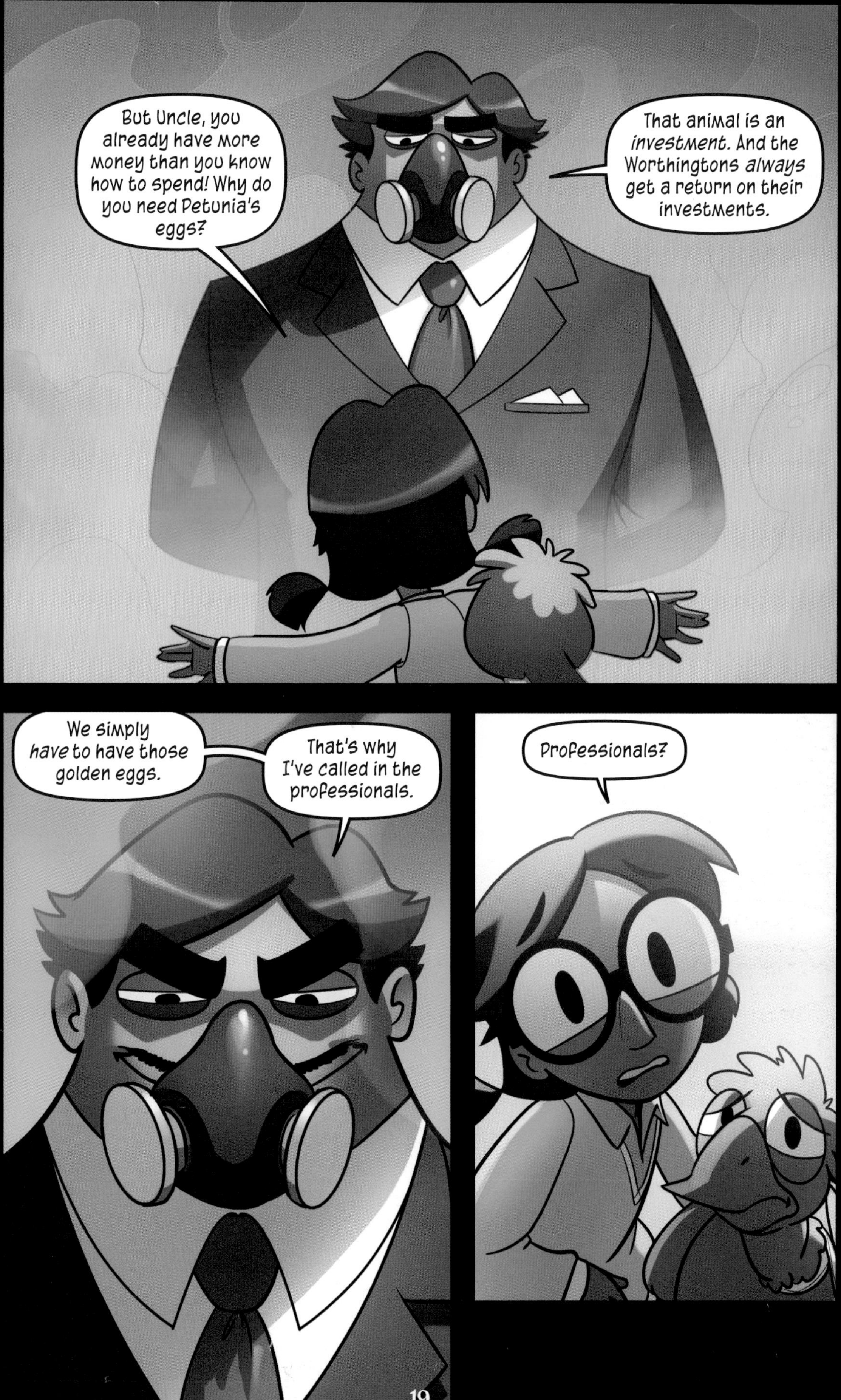
But Uncle, you already have more money than you know how to spend! Why do you need Petunia's eggs?
That animal is an *investment*. And the Worthingtons *always* get a return on their investments.
We simply *have* to have those golden eggs.
That's why I've called in the professionals.
Professionals?

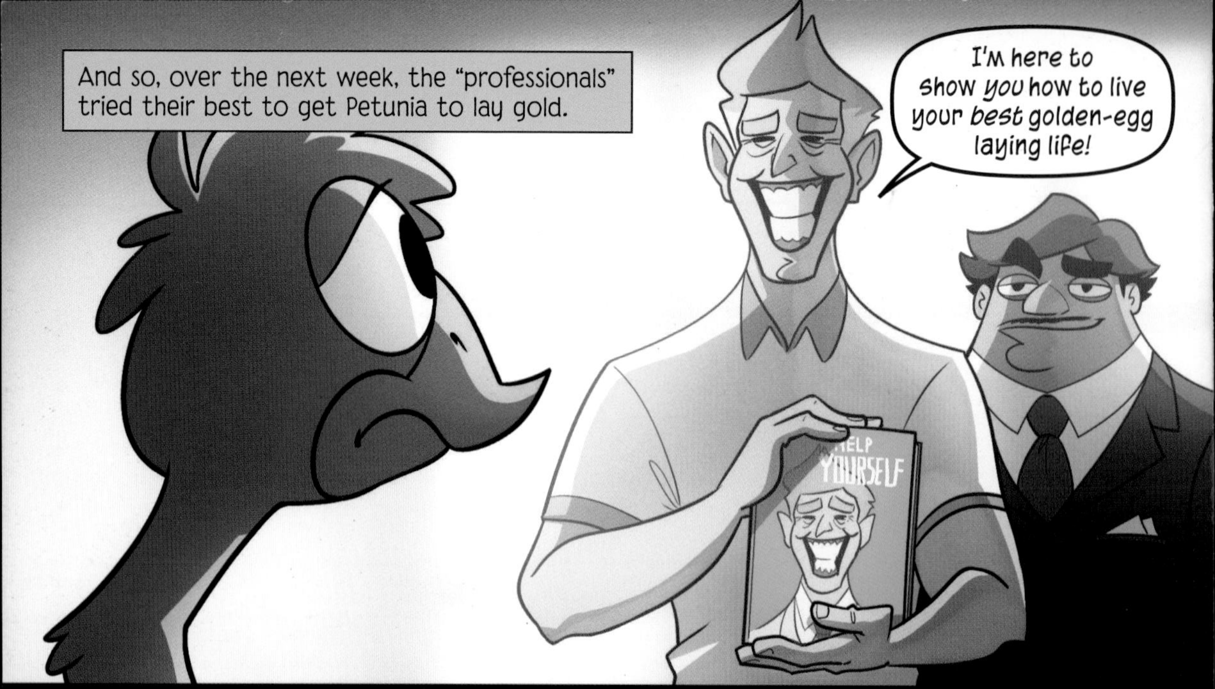
And so, over the next week, the "professionals" tried their best to get Petunia to lay gold.
I'm here to show you how to live your best golden-egg laying life!
HELP YOURSELF

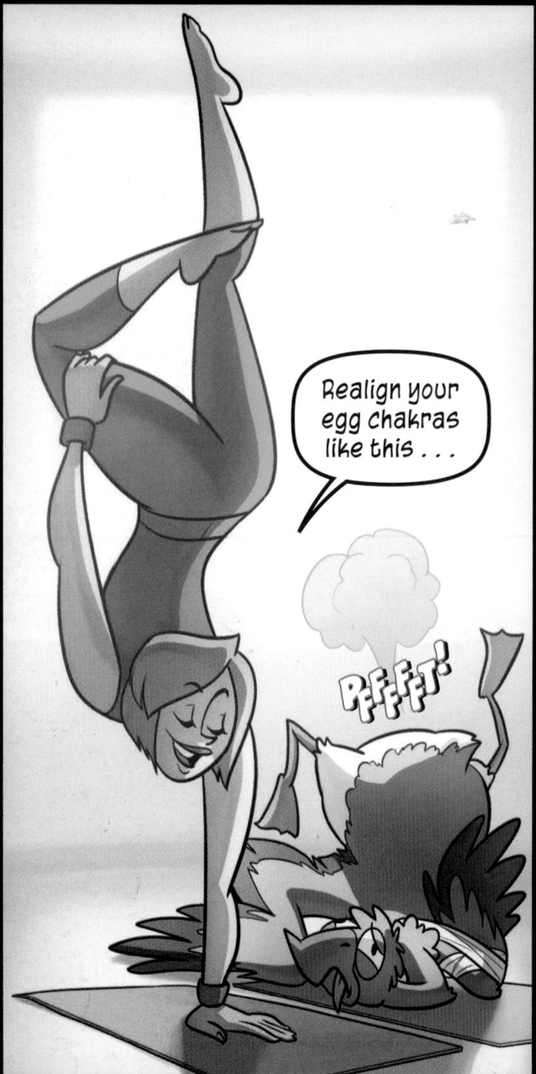
Realign your egg chakras like this . . .
PFFFFFT!

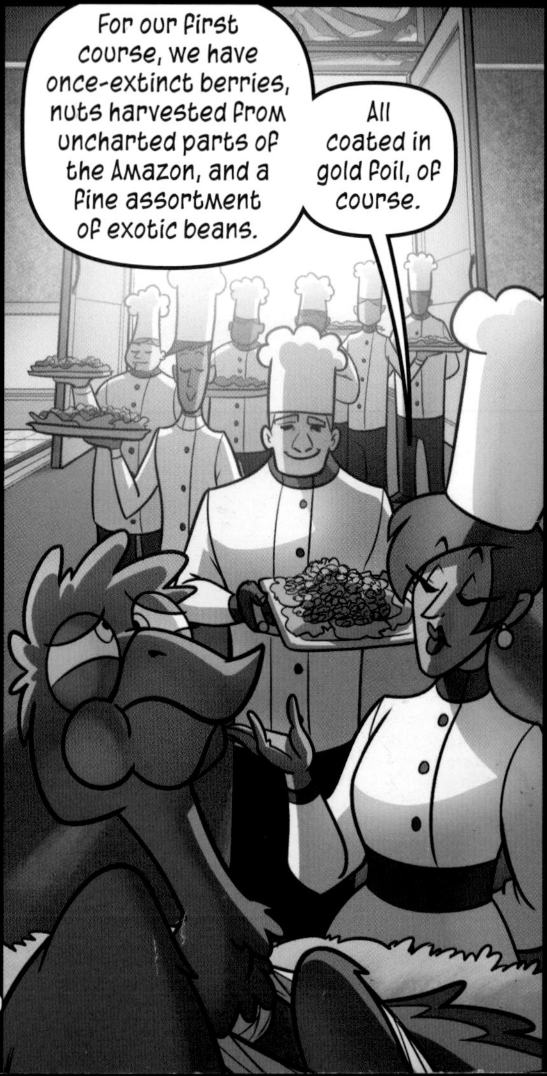
For our first course, we have once-extinct berries, nuts harvested from uncharted parts of the Amazon, and a fine assortment of exotic beans.
All coated in gold foil, of course.

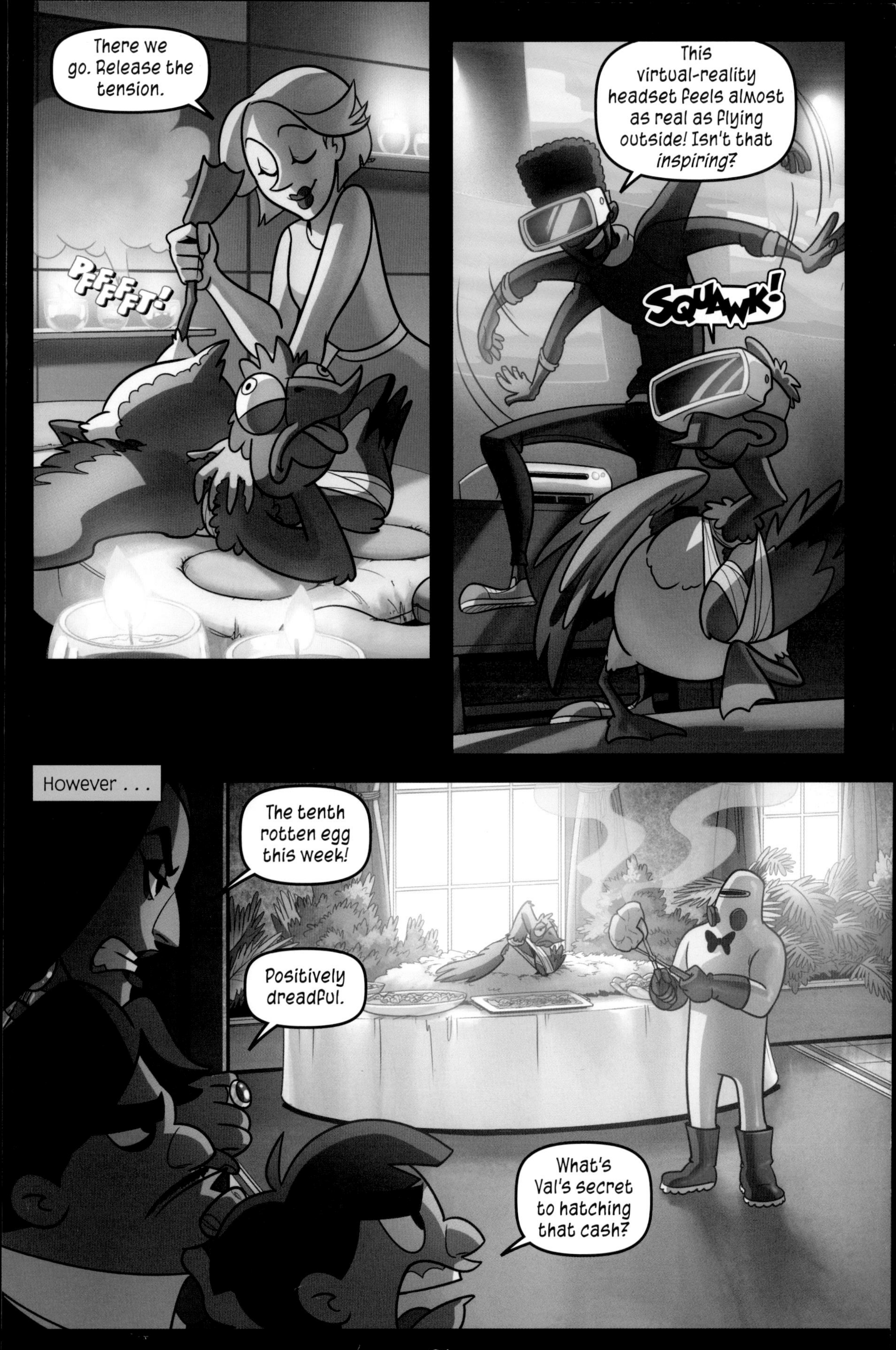
There we go. Release the tension.
PFFFFFT!
This virtual-reality headset feels almost as real as flying outside! Isn't that *inspiring*?
SQUAWK!
However . . .
The tenth rotten egg this week!
Positively dreadful.
What's Val's secret to hatching that cash?

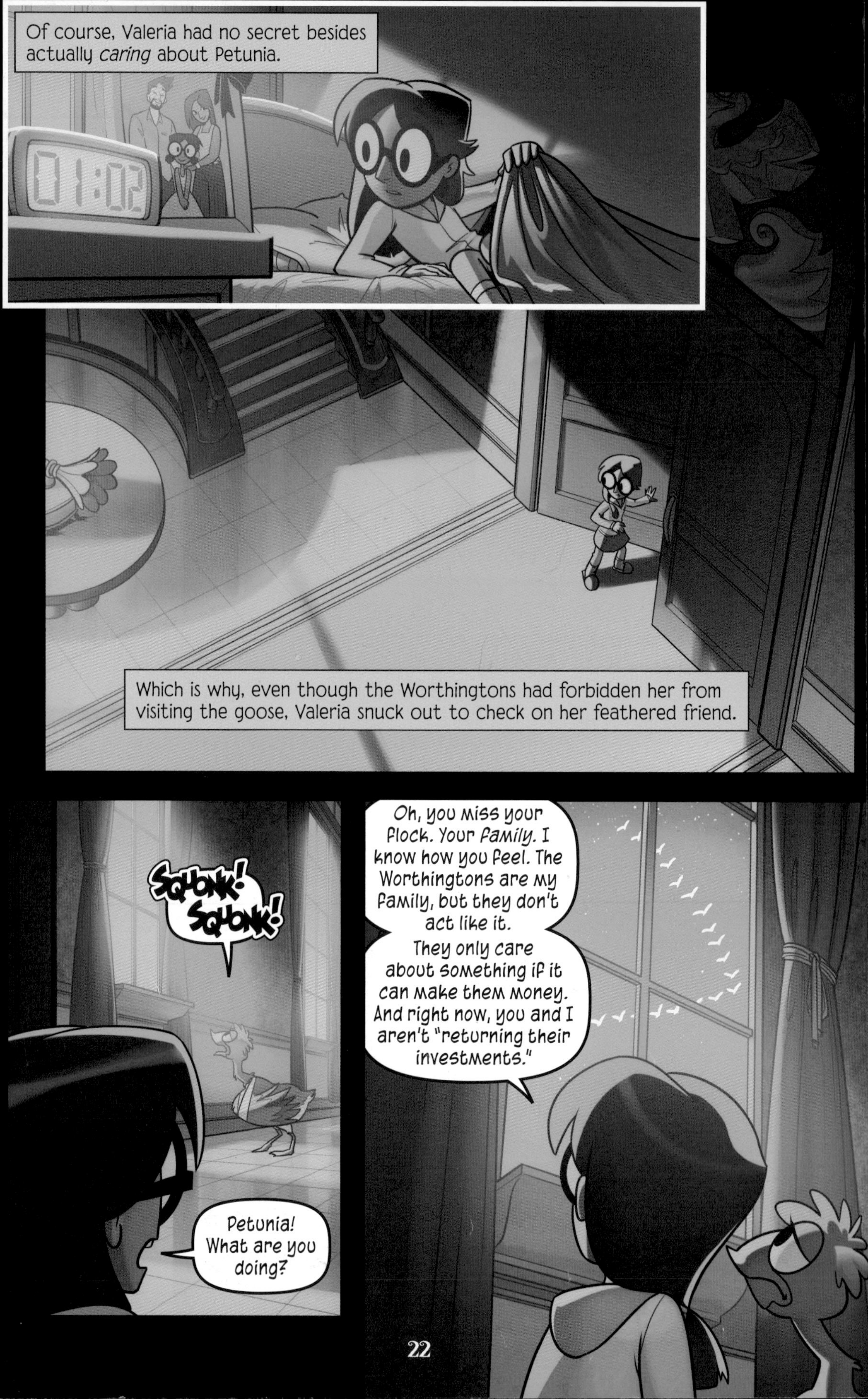

Of course, Valeria had no secret besides actually *caring* about Petunia.
01:02
Which is why, even though the Worthingtons had forbidden her from visiting the goose, Valeria snuck out to check on her feathered friend.
SQUONK! SQUONK!
Petunia! What are you doing?
Oh, you miss your flock. Your *family*. I know how you feel. The Worthingtons are my family, but they don't act like it.
They only care about something if it can make them money. And right now, you and I aren't "returning their investments."

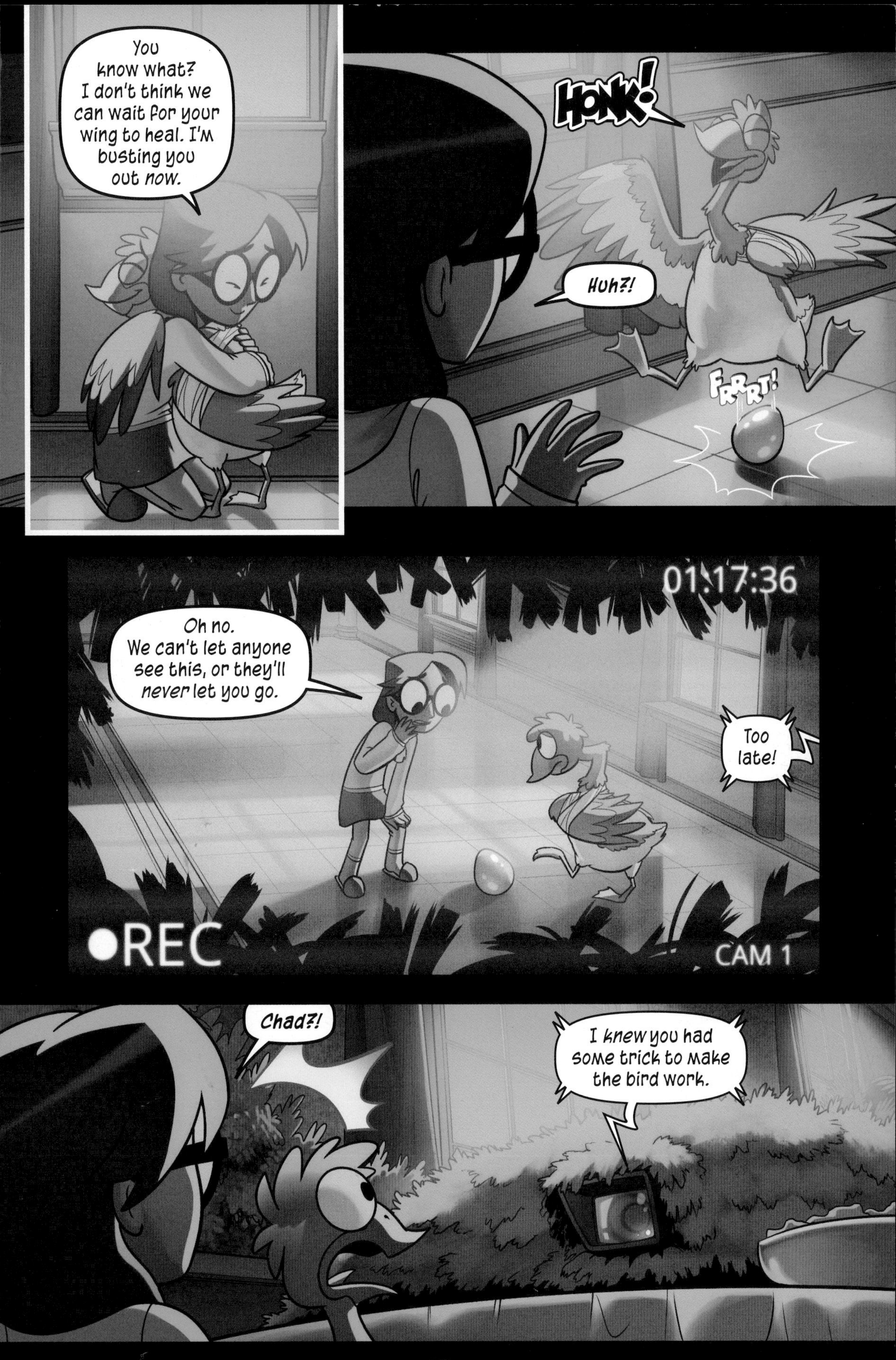
You know what? I don't think we can wait for your wing to heal. I'm busting you out now.
HONK!
Huh?!
FRRRT!
01:17:36
Oh no. We can't let anyone see this, or they'll never let you go.
Too late!
REC
CAM 1
Chad?!
I knew you had some trick to make the bird work.

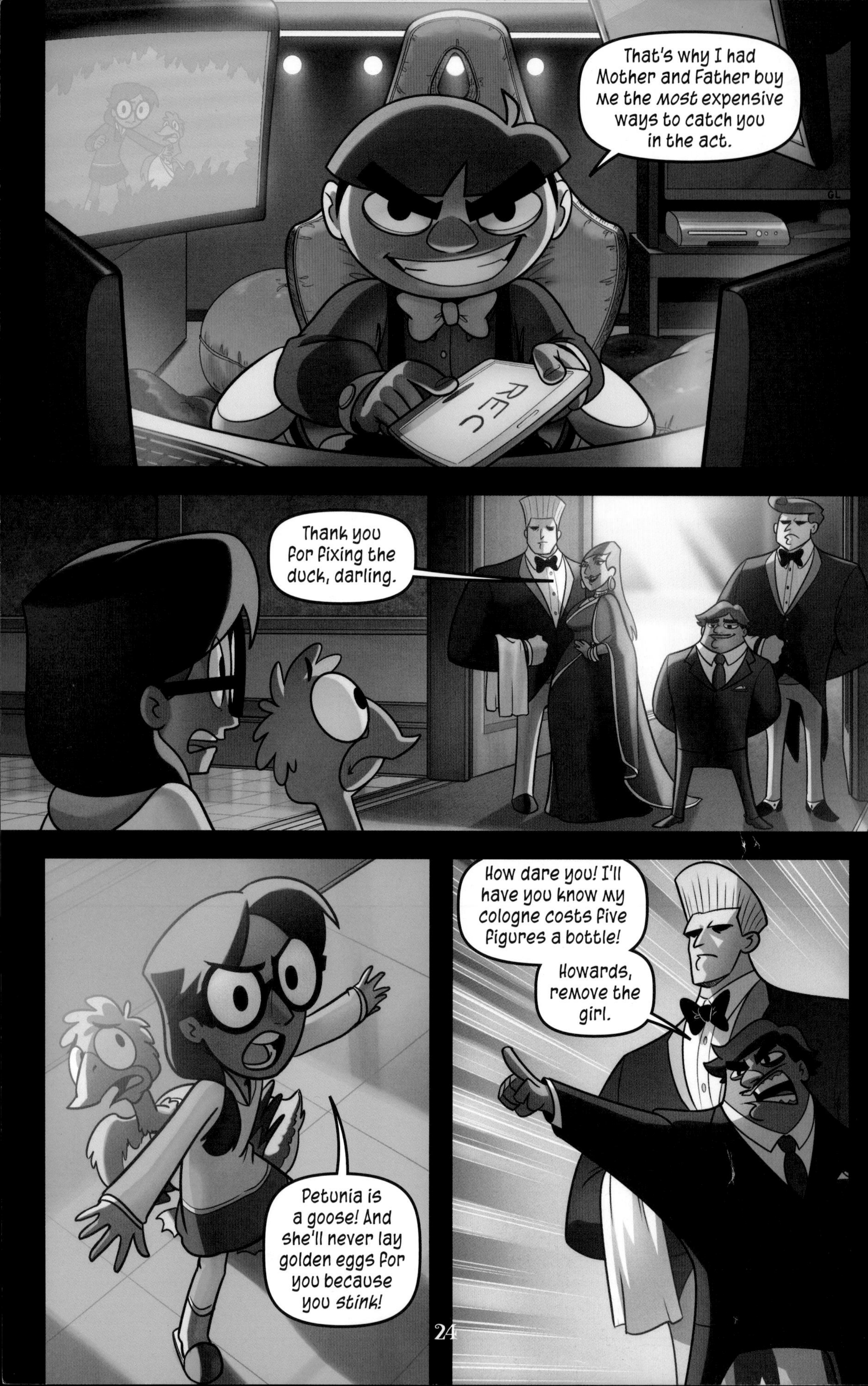
That's why I had Mother and Father buy me the *most* expensive ways to catch you in the act.
REC
GL
Thank you for fixing the duck, darling.
Petunia is a goose! And she'll never lay golden eggs for you because you *stink!*
How dare you! I'll have you know my cologne costs five figures a bottle!
Howards, remove the girl.

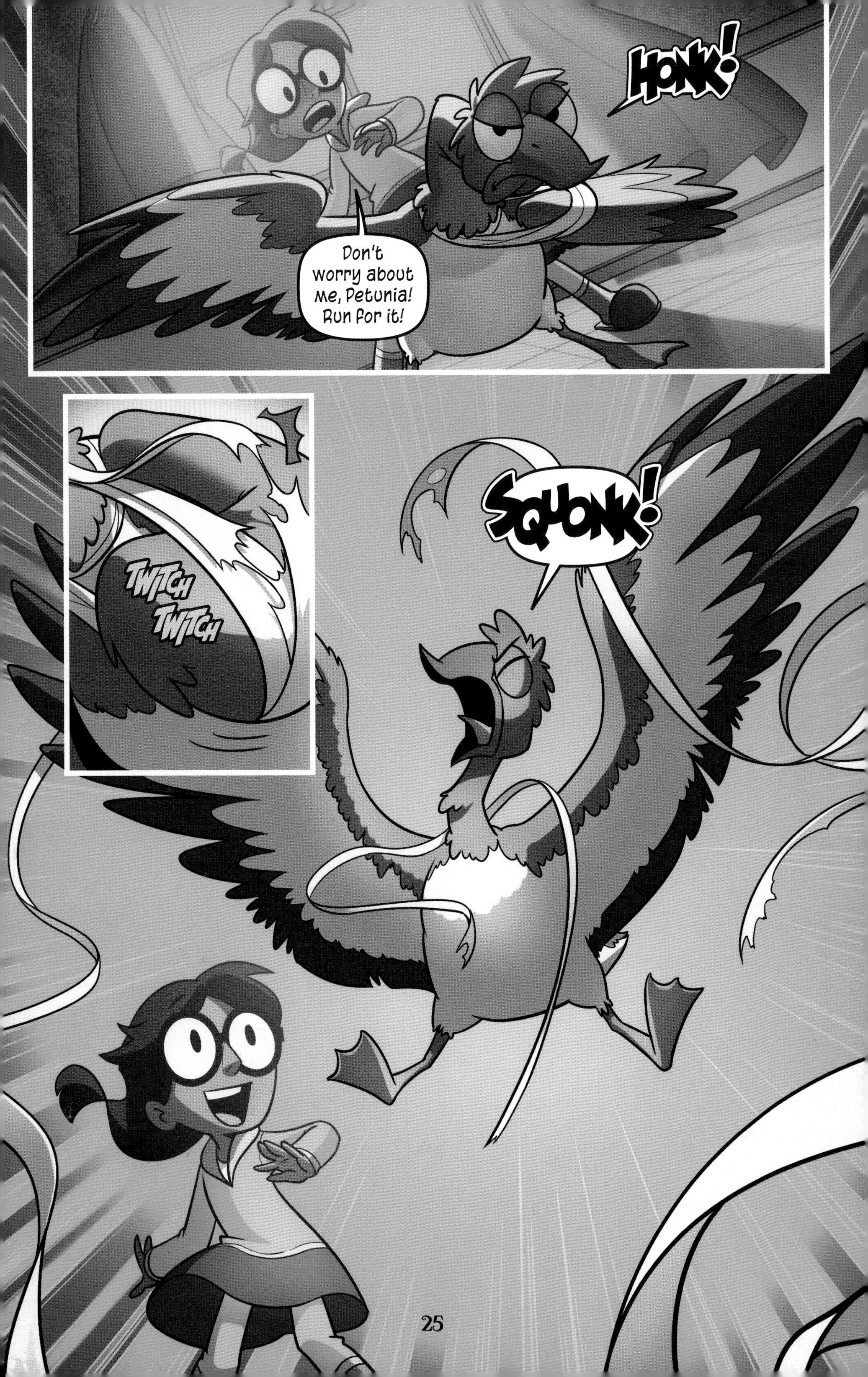
HONK!
Don't worry about me, Petunia! Run for it!
TWITCH
TWITCH
SQUONK!

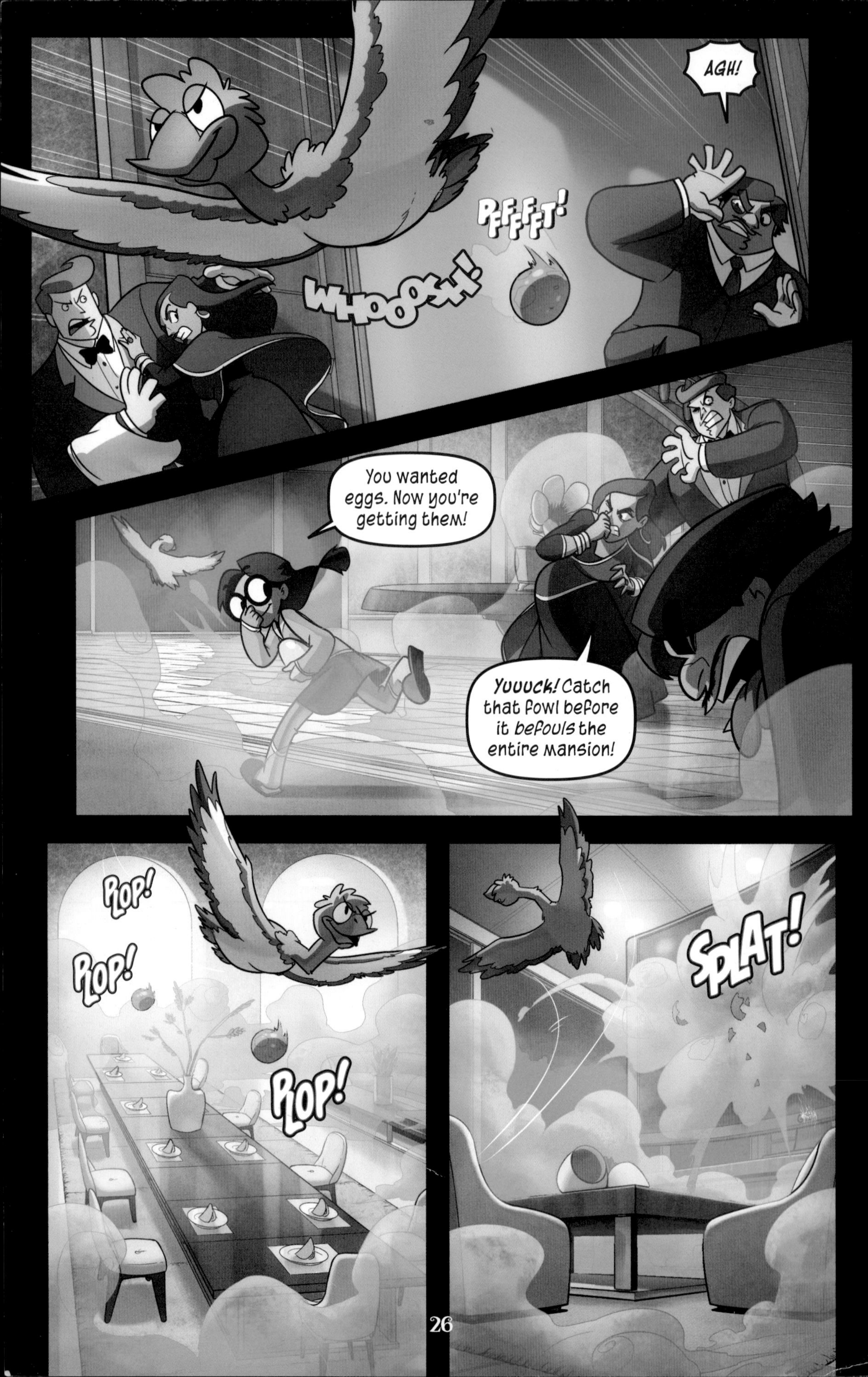
AGH!
PFFFFFT!
WHOOOSH!
You wanted eggs. Now you're getting them!
Yuuuck! Catch that fowl before it befouls the entire mansion!
PLOP!
PLOP!
PLOP!
SPLAT!

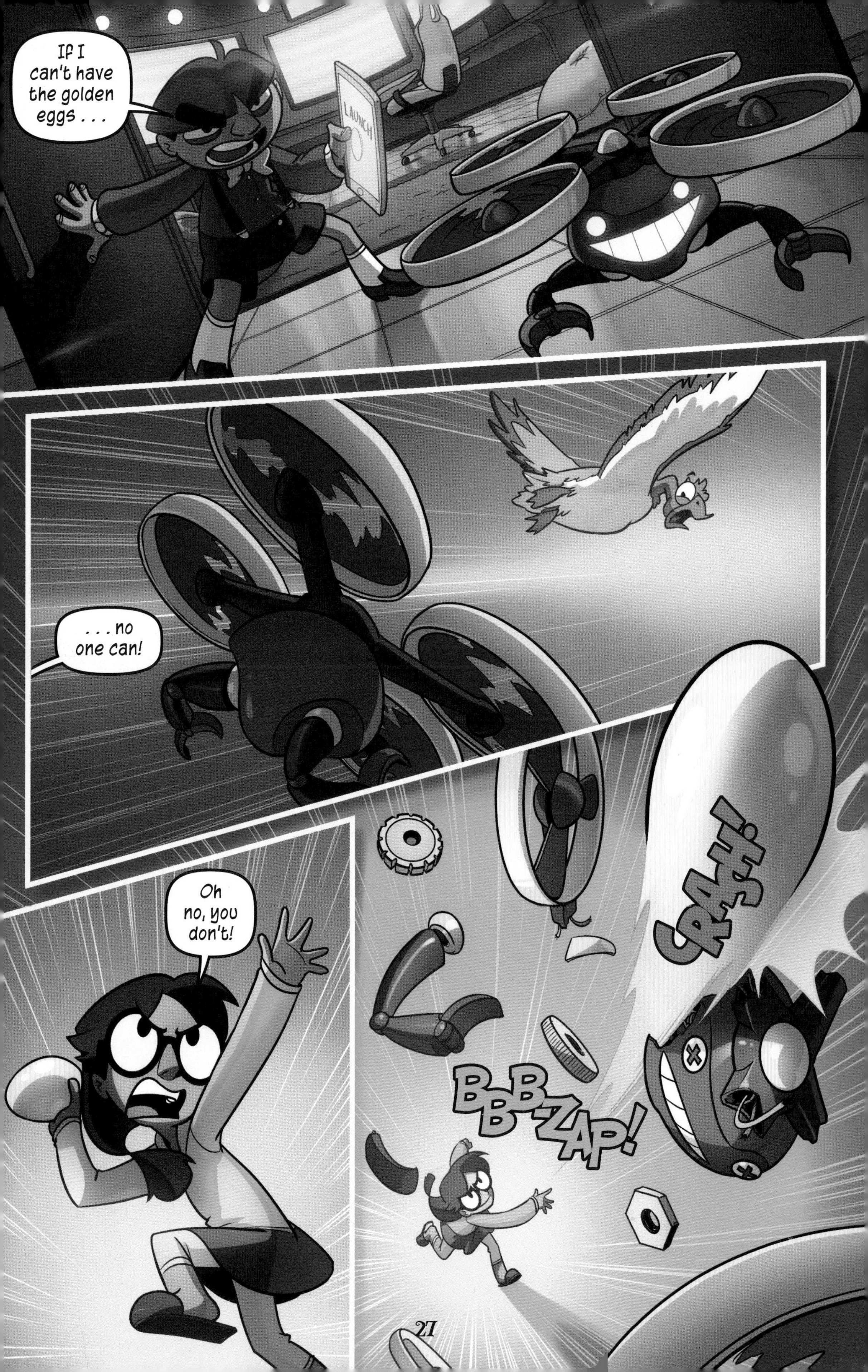
If I can't have the golden eggs . . .
LAUNCH
. . . no one can!
Oh no, you don't!
CRASH!
BBBZAP!

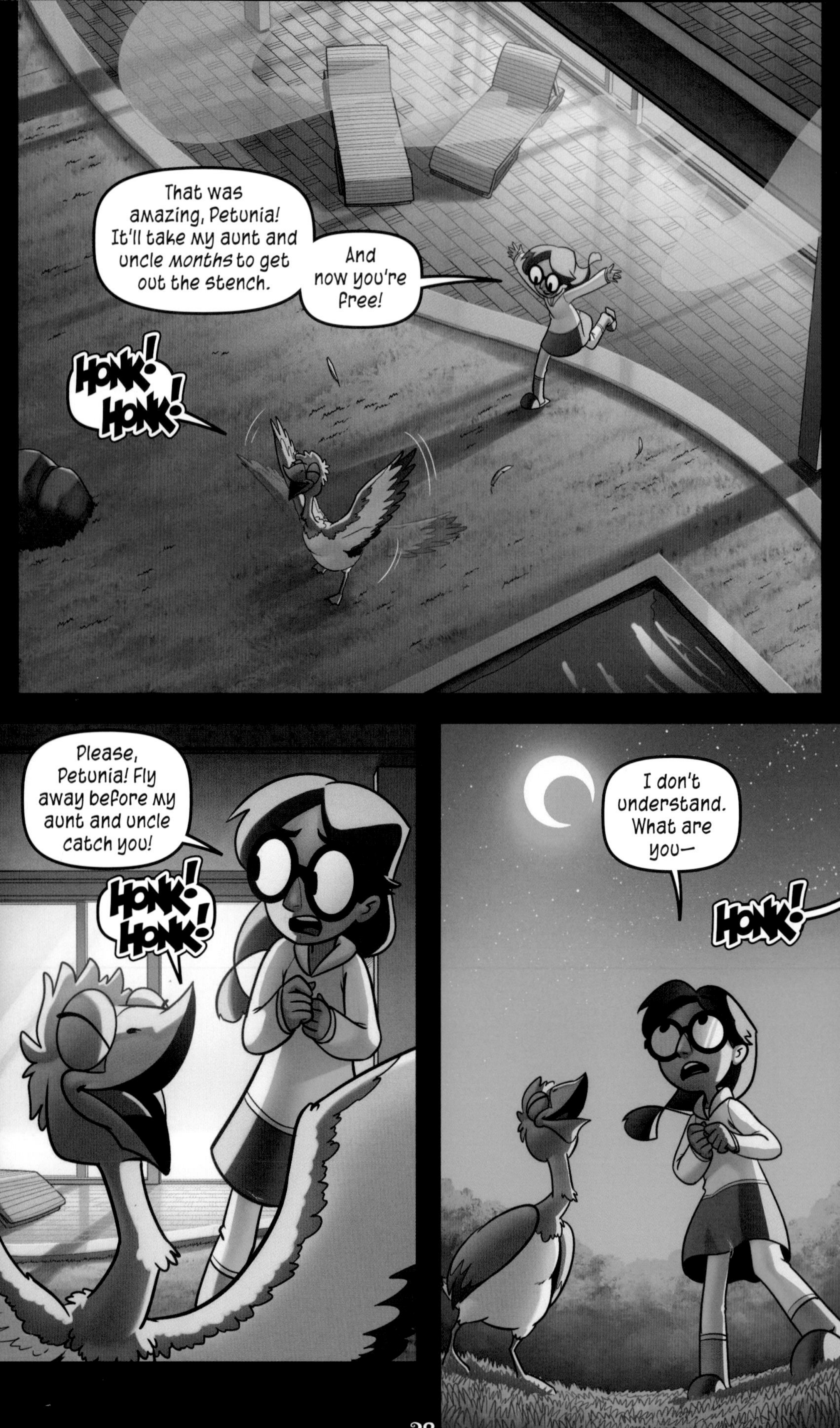
That was amazing, Petunia! It'll take my aunt and uncle *months* to get out the stench.
And now you're free!
HONK! HONK!
Please, Petunia! Fly away before my aunt and uncle catch you!
HONK! HONK!
I don't understand. What are you—
HONK!

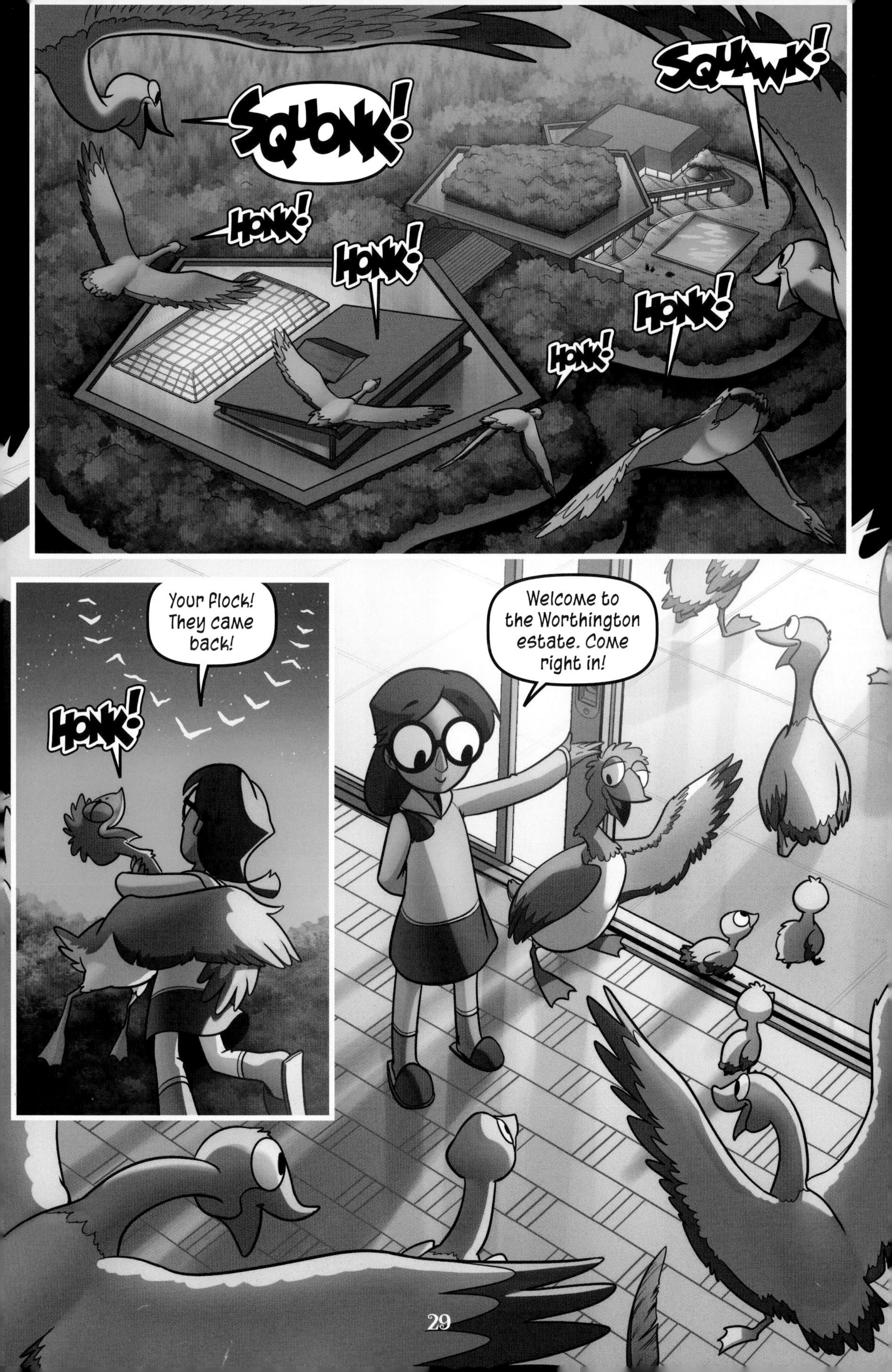
SQUONK!
SQUAWK!
HONK!
HONK!
HONK!
HONK!
Your flock! They came back!
HONK!
Welcome to the Worthington estate. Come right in!

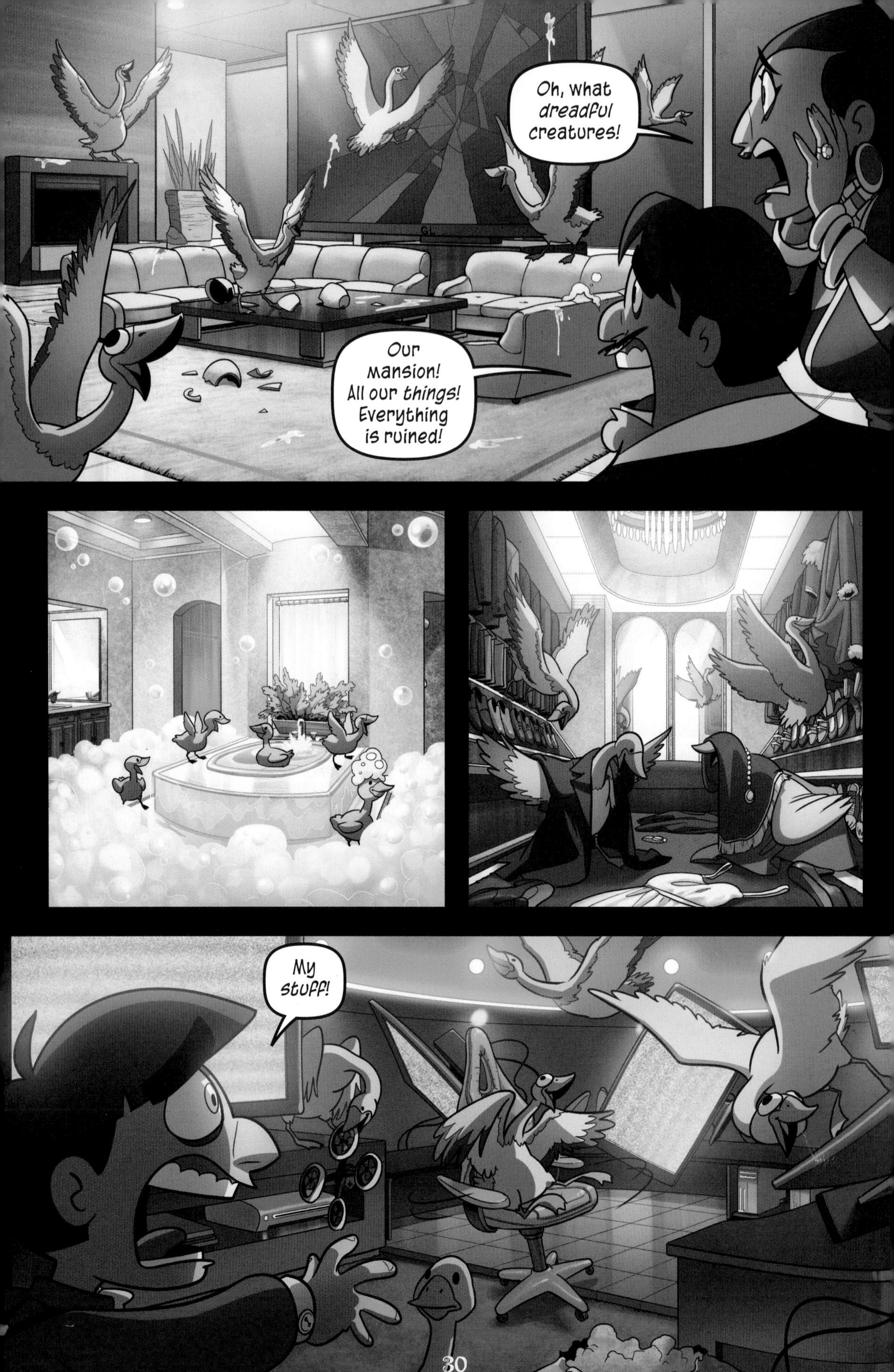
Oh, what *dreadful* creatures!
Our mansion! All our *things!* Everything is ruined!
My stuff!

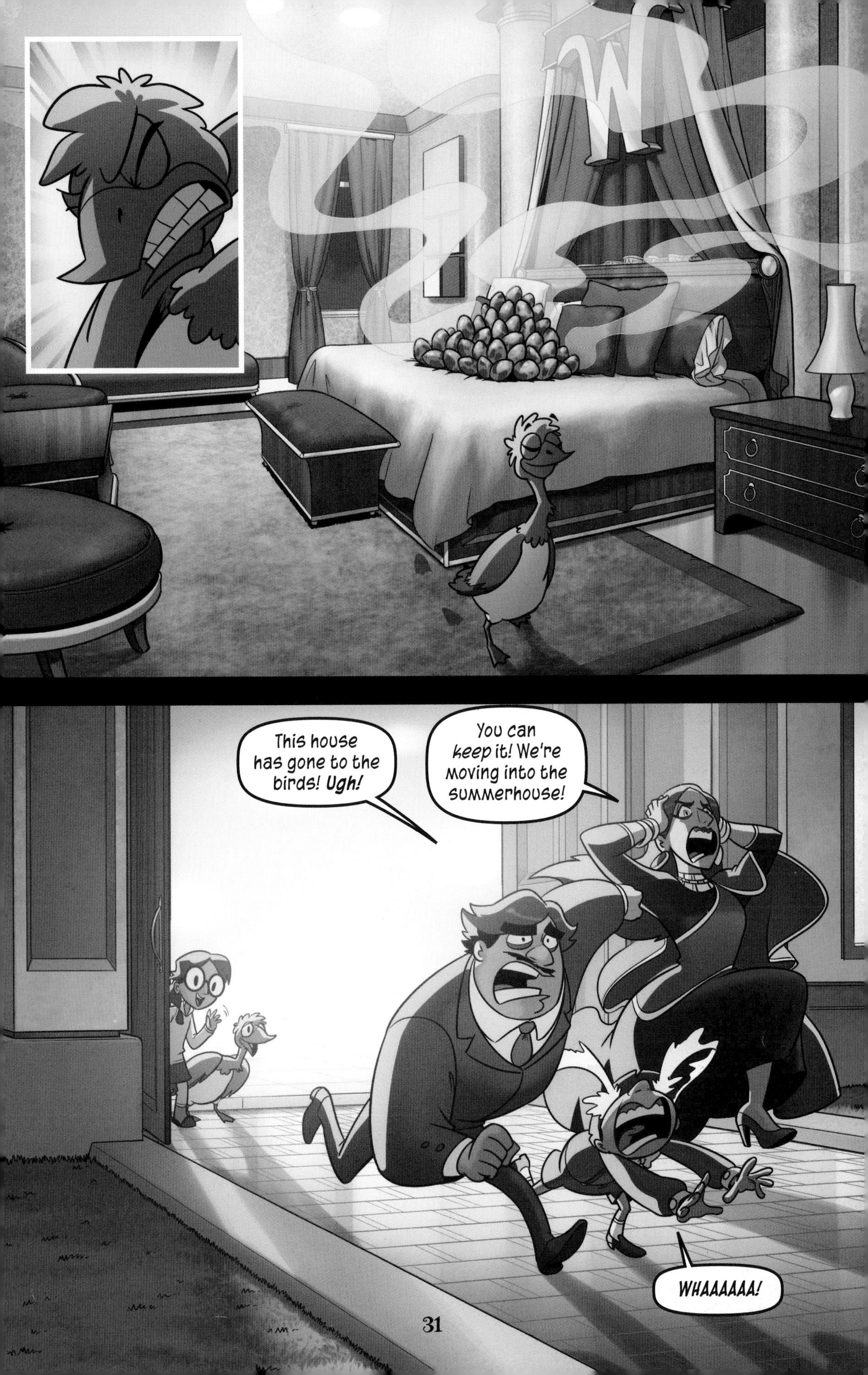
This house has gone to the birds! Ugh!
You can keep it! We're moving into the summerhouse!
WHAAAAAA!

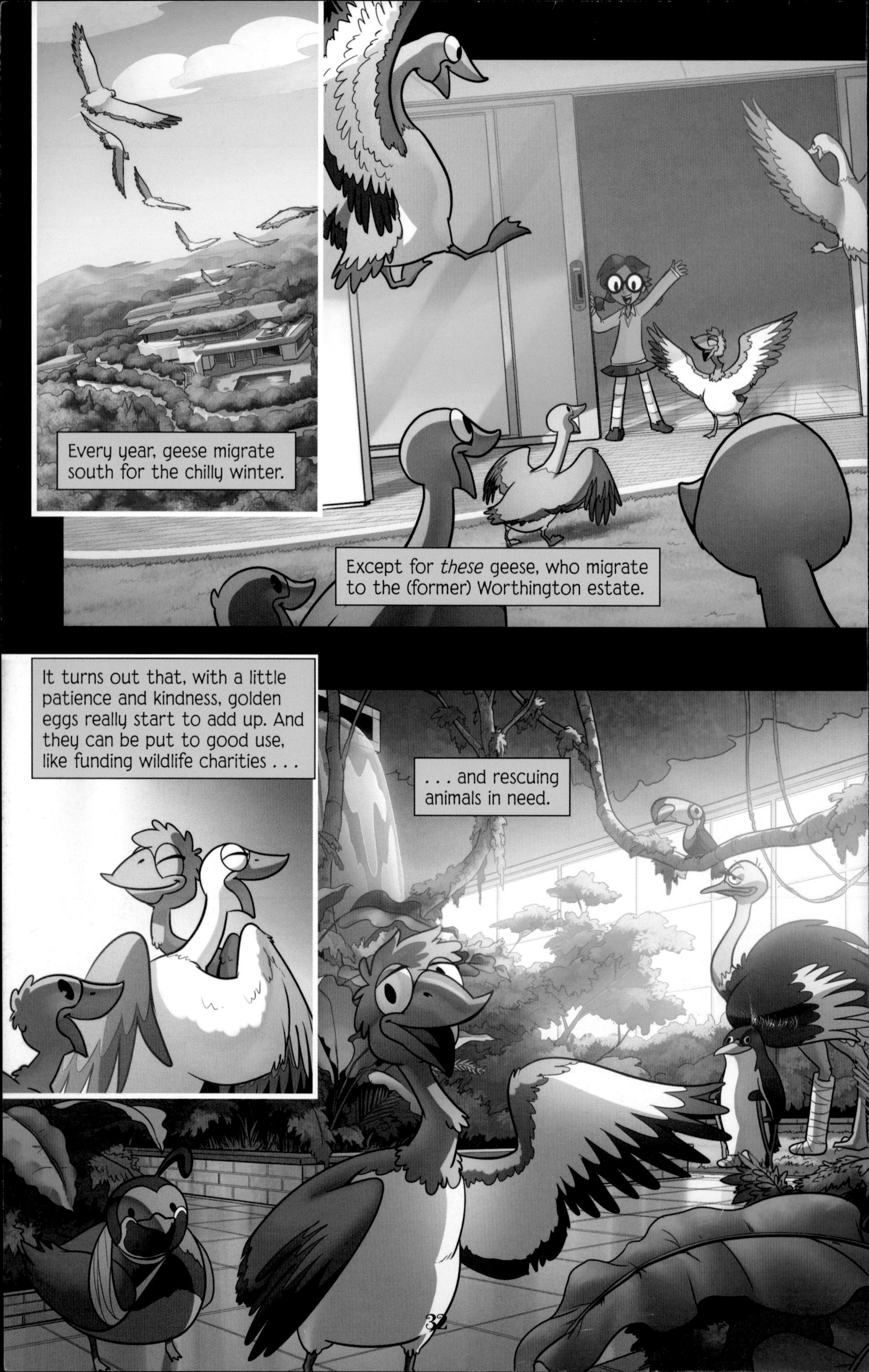
Every year, geese migrate south for the chilly winter.
Except for *these* geese, who migrate to the (former) Worthington estate.
It turns out that, with a little patience and kindness, golden eggs really start to add up. And they can be put to good use, like funding wildlife charities . . .
. . . and rescuing animals in need.

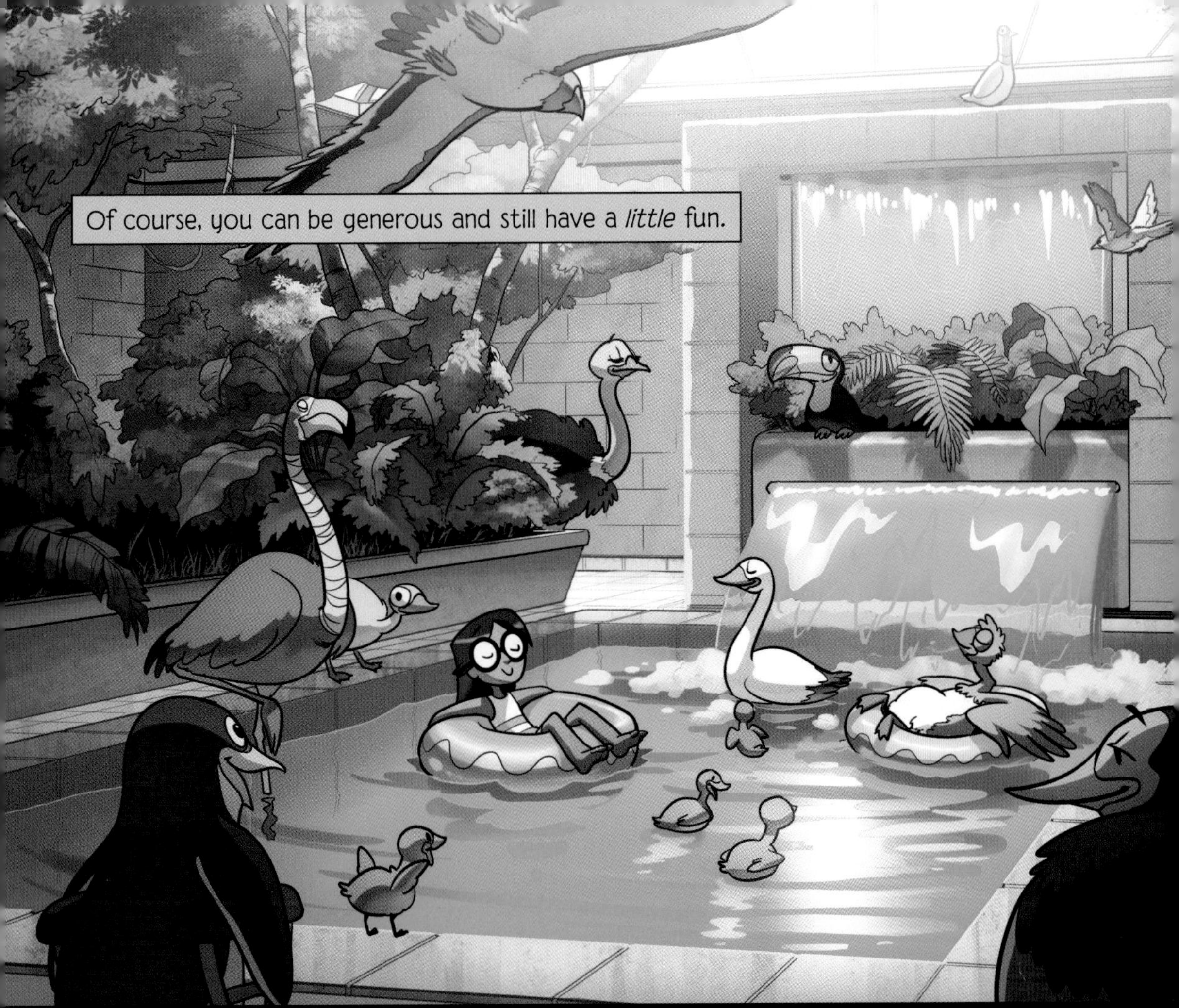
Of course, you can be generous and still have a *little* fun.

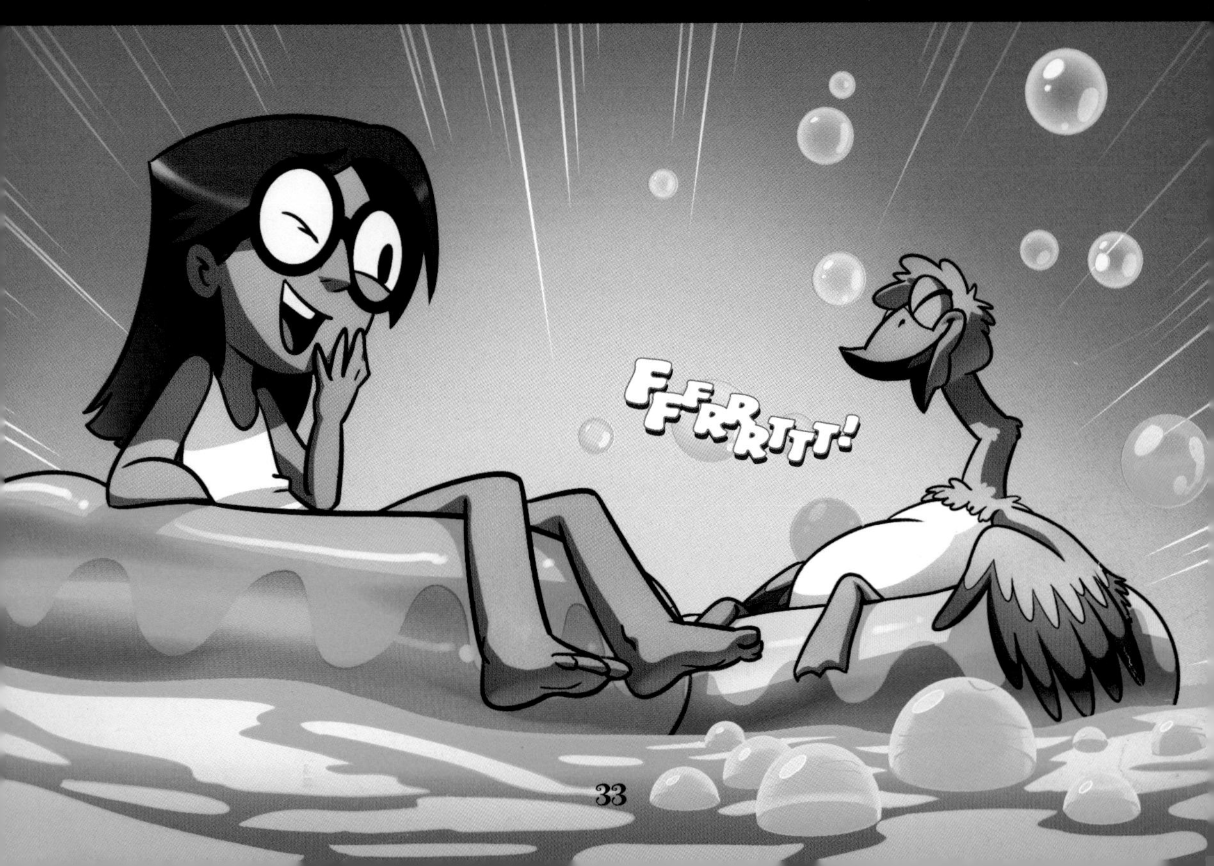
FFFRRRTTT!

ALL ABOUT FABLES

A fable is a short tale that teaches the reader a lesson about life, often with animal characters. Most fables were first told thousands of years ago by a Greek storyteller named Aesop. At the end of a fable, there's almost always a moral (a fancy word for lesson) stated right out so you don't miss it. Yes, fables can be kind of bossy, but they usually give pretty good advice. Read on to learn more about Aesop's original fable and its moral. Can you spot any other lessons?

THE GOOSE THAT LAID THE GOLDEN EGG

One day, a farmer and his wife were overjoyed to discover that their goose had laid a shining, sparkling, glittery gold egg! Each day, the goose laid another solid-gold egg. And each day, the farmer and his wife sold the egg at the market. Before long, the couple was quite rich. But they also grew impatient that the goose laid only one egg a day. They wanted to get even richer, even faster. So the farmer decided to cut the goose open and collect all the golden eggs at once. But when he looked inside the goose, he didn't find a single egg. Because of their greed, the couple lost their goose—and all of the gold they would have received if they had just been patient.

THE MORAL

GREED OVERREACHES ITSELF
(In other words, being greedy often backfires, ruining what made you happy in the first place!)

A **FAR OUT** GUIDE TO THE FABLE'S STINKY TWISTS!

The eggs Petunia lays aren't always solid gold. She can also drop ones that are extra-stinky and rotten!

In the original, the goose doesn't have friends. In this story, Val lends a helping hand, and so does Petunia's flock!

Instead of cutting the goose open (yikes!), the Worthingtons try all sorts of ways to get more gold eggs, from pricey foods to yoga classes.

The goose meets a sad fate in Aesop's version. Here, Petunia rejoins her flock and her gold eggs are put to good use.

VISUAL QUESTIONS

Why did some of Petunia's eggs come out rotten? Use examples from the text and art to back up your answer.

1

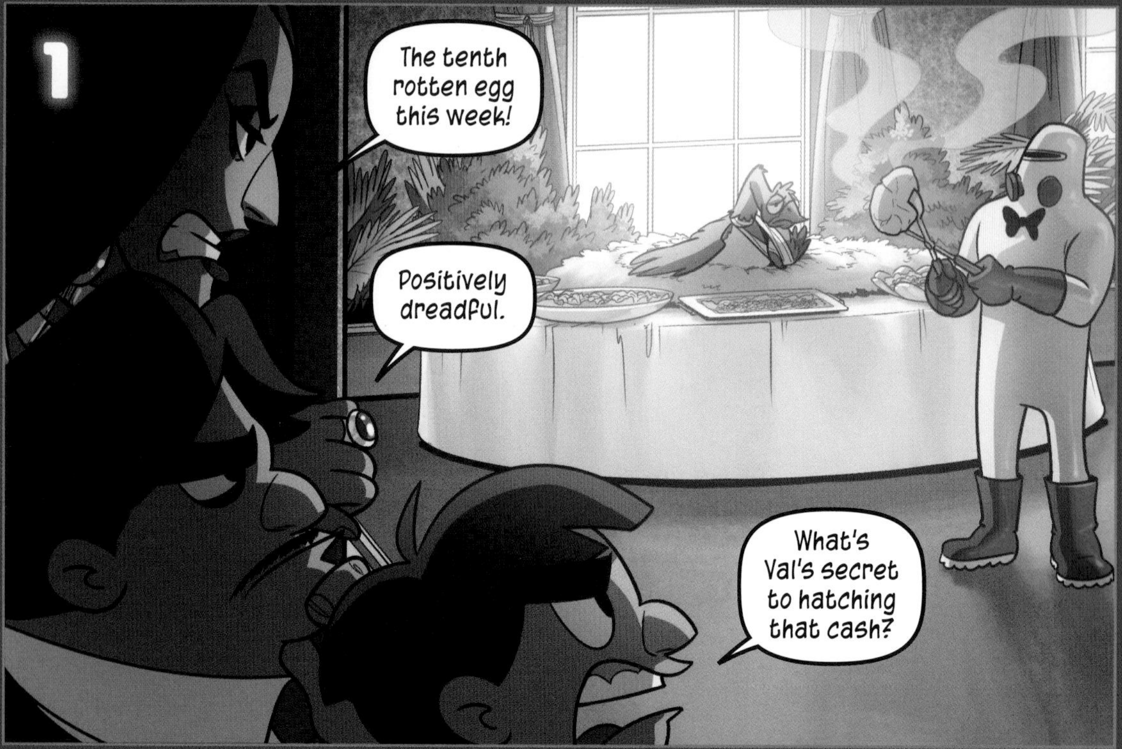
The tenth rotten egg this week!
Positively dreadful.
What's Val's secret to hatching that cash?

This frame on page 13 isn't like others. Why? Who is watching Val? How do you know? Look for other spots in the story that use unique frames.

2

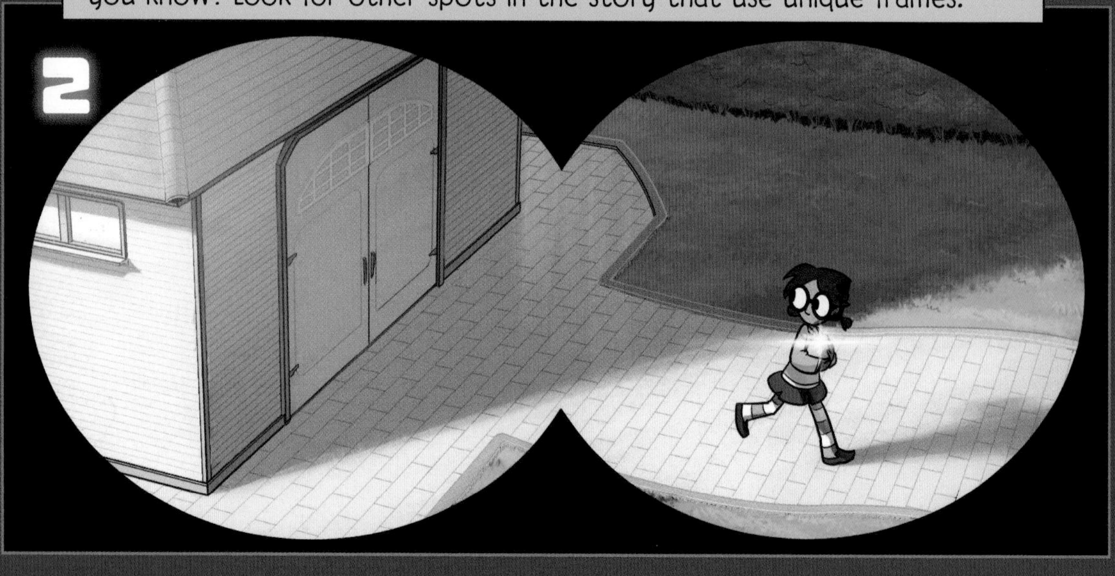

These panels from page 8 are set up side by side. How are Valeria's and Chad's reactions similar? How are they different? What does the moment tell you about their characters?

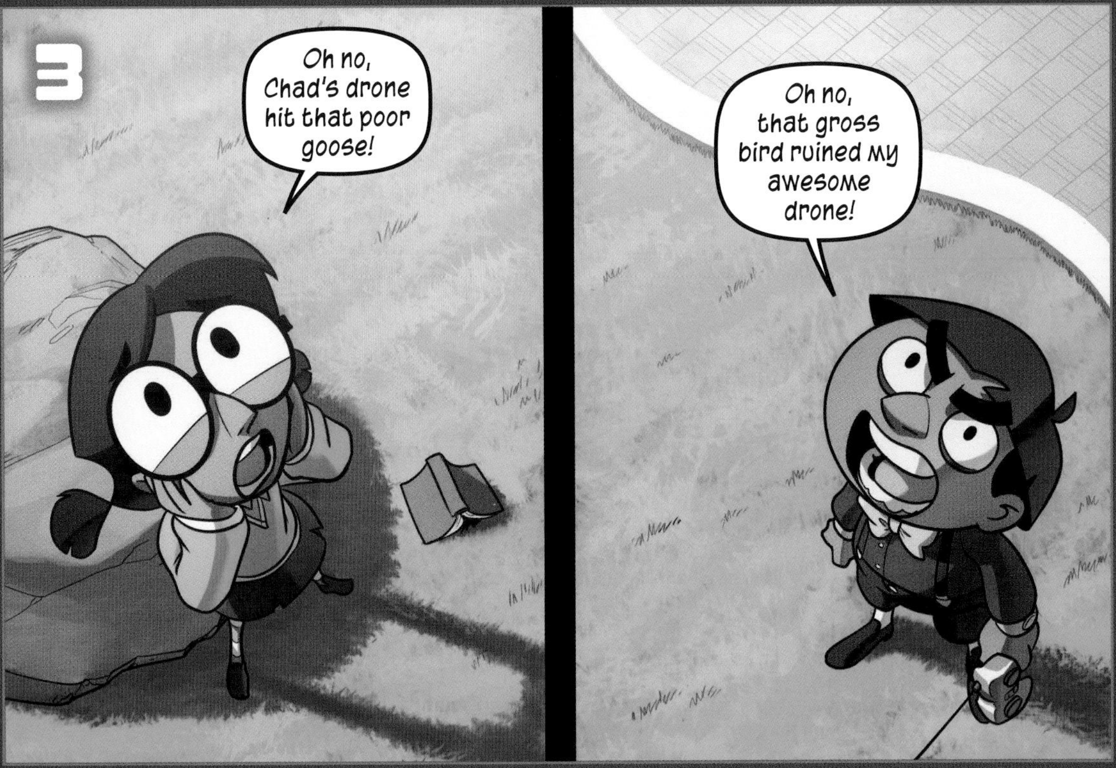
3
Oh no, Chad's drone hit that poor goose!
Oh no, that gross bird ruined my awesome drone!

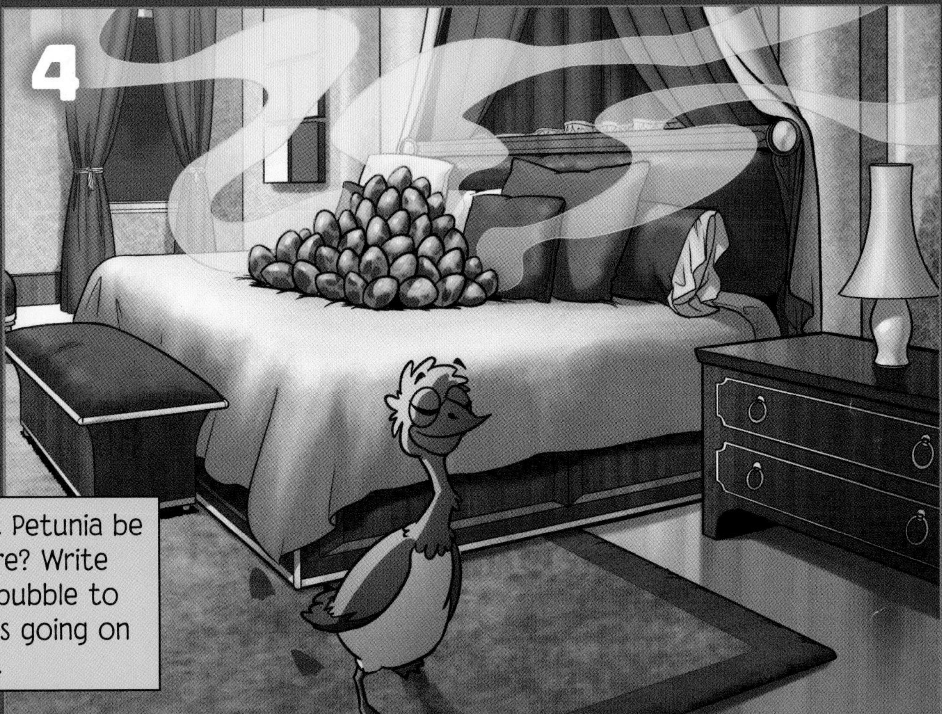
4

What might Petunia be thinking here? Write a thought bubble to show what's going on in her mind.

AUTHOR

Steve Foxe is the author of more than 50 children's books and comics for properties including Pokémon, Batman, Transformers, Adventure Time, Steven Universe, and Grumpy Cat. He lives in Queens, New York. He doesn't eat eggs, but wouldn't say no to receiving a golden one once in a while.

ILLUSTRATOR

Fern Cano is an illustrator born in Mexico City, Mexico. He currently resides in Monterrey, Mexico, where he makes a living as an illustrator and colorist. He has done work for Marvel, DC Comics, and role-playing games like Pathfinder from Paizo Publishing. In his spare time, he enjoys hanging out with friends, singing, rowing, and drawing!

GLOSSARY

befoul (bih-FOWL)—to make something dirty

chakra (CHUHK-ruh)—in yoga, a point of physical and spiritual energy inside the body

cologne (kuh-LOHN)—a nice-smelling liquid that people put on their skin

drone (DROHN)—a small aircraft that is controlled by remote

estate (eh-STAYT)—a large area of land that usually has a big house on it

fowl (FOWL)—any type of bird

fund (FUHND)—money that is put aside and saved for a special purpose; to provide money for something

generous (JEN-er-uhs)—sharing or giving things because you want to and showing kindness toward others

investment (in-VEST-muhnt)—something you have spent money on with the hope that it will eventually make you more money

migrate (MYE-grayt)—to go from one place to another at different times of the year

return (rih-TURN)—the money made from an investment

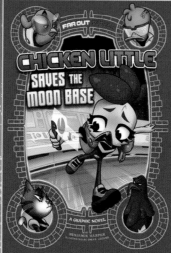
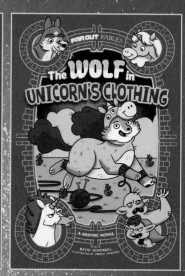